A SMALL SECRET

AMISH ROMANCE SECRETS BOOK 3

SAMANTHA PRICE

CHAPTER 1

Yea, though I walk through the valley of the shadow of death,
I will fear no evil: for thou art with me;
thy rod and thy staff they comfort me.
Psalm 23:4

NORMALLY SARAH LIKED TO COOK, but tonight baked breaded lamb chops were on the menu and the smell rising from the meat as it sizzled in the pan, sent Sarah rushing for the outdoor convenience. She thought it was called 'morning sickness' because it happened only in the morning. No one had told her it could happen throughout the day as well. In fact, for Sarah, it seemed to be happening all through the day. She considered that it should be called 'all day sickness' rather than morning sickness.

After she was finished being sick, she quickly splashed her face with the icy cold November water that flowed from the well around the back of the house. As she usually did after one of these episodes, she plucked a sprig of fresh mint and popped it in her mouth, as she made her way back to the kitchen. Mint was the only thing that Sarah could find to settle her nausea.

As Sarah pushed the back door open, her *mudder* who had her hands on her hips, and a very sour expression on her face met her. *Oh no, she's figured it out. She knows I'm expecting. Nee, she couldn't possibly know for sure I'm not even showing yet,* she thought. The only clue of her early pregnancy was the terrible nausea that she'd had for a little over two weeks.

"It's that dreaded flu, Sarah. Were you sick again this time?"

Sarah nodded her head at her *mudder's* question pleased that her secret was still safe, but not pleased that she had to keep this secret from her parents. However did she get herself into this situation? If Sarah had heard that someone else in the community was not married and expecting a *boppli* she would have had a very low opinion of them indeed, and now, here she was in that very same situation.

Thankfully, the flu was going around the community and many were quite ill, so that gave her a good cover up story for the moment.

Her mother put the back of her hand to Sarah's forehead. "You don't seem to have a temperature though."

Sarah barely had the strength to speak, but managed to say, "That's *gut.*"

"Go up to bed and I'll bring dinner up to you."

Dinner was the last thing that Sarah felt like. The last thing in the world she wanted to think about was food. She couldn't arouse suspicion and tell her *mudder* that she wasn't hungry and besides her *mudder's* tone was firm and Sarah did not have the strength to argue. She was thankful that at least she would be able to hide in the safety of her room and wouldn't have to smell the meat cooking any longer. "*Denke, mamm.*"

As she carefully made her way up the stairs to her bedroom, she wondered if her mother suspected her condition. She was sure she saw her eyes flicker toward her slightly swollen belly. *Was she checking to see if my belly is increasing? Or maybe it's my guilty conscience*, she thought. Either way, Sarah was glad to be able to lie down because when she was lying down she didn't feel quite as sick.

Her *mudder* called after her. "I'll make you some hot lemon and honey." Hot lemon and honey in boiling water was the standard remedy her *mudder* used for everything, not just a cold or the flu, it was her standard cure for everything.

"Denke, Mamm." *One squeezed fresh lemon, two tablespoons full of honey in a mug of boiling water, Jah that will cure everything. If only it were as simple as that,* Sarah thought. *If only I could take the honey and lemon drink and I wouldn't be in this situation anymore.*

There was no cure for what Sarah had. Sarah realized that for the first time in her life this is something she could not change her mind about and something that she could not get out of. She could not change her mind on a whim and say she didn't want to be an unmarried expectant mother anymore. It wasn't like a game of volleyball where she could stop playing whenever she wished and have someone else take over. It wasn't like school where she could pretend she was sick and stay home. Everything Sarah could think of in her life up to this point she had always been able to change her mind about or find some way out of. These circumstances were different.

Why couldn't her life be plain and simple like her two older sisters'? They were both happy to stay and live within the Amish community and had both fallen in love with Amish *menner*. One was about to be married and the other was already happily married with a *boppli* on the way.

That's the trouble, Sarah thought, *with having two older sisters, the younger one is supposed to turn out just like the older ones, just as if they were cut from the same cookie cutter.* Sarah felt she had dismally failed to live up to the life that her older sisters were leading. *I guess the problem was that Benjamin and Jessie didn't have a younger bruder;* she tried to see the funny side of things as her two sisters had married two *bruders* who they had practically grown up with. Yet, she had to be the one to fall in love with an *Englisher.*

Sarah sighed loudly as she thought of how her older sisters always had things work out so well for them. She could already see that her life would be hard in comparison with theirs. *Nothing ever seems to work out easily for me*, she thought. *I fell in love with John as soon as I looked into his blue eyes.*

She closed her eyes and remembered that first time she gazed into his eyes and felt lost in his presence. Nothing in the world up to that point had given her the feeling of elation as John spoke his first words to her. She didn't even remember what he said; she could only remember how her heart seemed to dance as if nothing in the whole entire world mattered at all. *It was too late for my heart to disregard him for being an Englischer. When he told me that first night that he wasn't really Amish, and was just visiting his Amish cousin, we were already deeply in love.*

Even though it was mighty chilly outside, Sarah pushed up her bedroom window just a little, for the fresh air that always made her feel better. She stood in front of the window even though the cold wind was sending chills up and down her spine. Sarah took several deep breaths before she closed it and sank into the coziness of her familiar bed. As she placed her head on the softness of her pillow, her hand automatically reached for the well-worn photo of John she kept under the pillow. The photo had been inside his very first letter to her and she had gazed at it longingly every day since.

The photo was nice to have for now so she could see his handsome face anytime she wanted to, but Sarah longed to be able to see him in person again very soon. She craved to look into his deep blue eyes and to have his strong protective arms around her once more. She didn't know why she felt about him the way she did, it was just that everything seemed a lot better when he was around.

Sarah ran the tip of her finger over his face then drew the photo to her lips and kissed it.

She let out a large sigh. They only had two short months together, but in those two months they saw each other every single day. At first Sarah was pleasantly attracted to his handsome looks, but then as she got to know him, his personality far outshone his looks. Sarah had found herself also attracted to his intelligence. Compared to Amish *menner* John was able to speak on a whole range of topics and he had even travelled to different countries. Sarah loved to hear him talk of his adventures on his travels. In comparison Sarah thought Amish *menner* dull as they never go anywhere and just do the same thing over and over again.

Sarah wanted the life that she saw she could have with him. Since Sarah, like most Amish, only had a grade eight education, John said he would show her how to get her GED so she could go to college and have a career. Sarah had never even known these things were possible before she'd met John. Being a *gut fraa* bringing up well-behaved children and keeping her husband happy was the life Sarah had previously envisioned for herself. John inspired her to want to see what she was capable of in the *Englisch* world, but now with the *boppli* coming Sarah knew she had to re-think all of her previous plans. The *boppli* had become Sarah's main priority.

CHAPTER 2

"Do not be afraid. Do not be discouraged, for the Lord your God
will be with you wherever you go."
Joshua 1:9

"Sarah, can I come in."

Sarah quickly pushed the picture of John back under her pillow at the sound of Liz's voice and sat up. Liz had grown up Amish, but was now very much *Englisch*. Circumstances had caused Liz to be a long-term houseguest of the Millers.

"Sarah Miller, you may have fooled your mother with that little performance, but you haven't fooled me."

Liz put the mug of hot lemon and honey drink that she had been sent up with, down on the small nightstand next to the bed.

"Liz, I'm not sure what you mean." Sarah's heart was thumping. She was not ready to tell anyone. Even her two sisters Kate and Annie didn't know her secret. She hadn't told her *schweschder*, Kate, because she was expecting her own *boppli* in a few months and her other *schweschder*, Annie,

SAMANTHA PRICE

was just weeks away from her wedding. Sarah didn't want to burden either of her sisters with news of her sorry situation at such important and joyful times in their own lives.

Liz curled a long lock of bleached blonde hair around her perfectly manicured long pink fingernails. "Ahh, let me see. Two months ago you ran away with a man. A man you were ready to give up your family for and a man who you were willing to give up being Amish for, a man who you professed to love above all else. Now weeks later, you start throwing up and can't stand to be around cooking smells."

Liz stopped to draw a breath and sat down on the end of Sarah's bed. "I've known you for most of your life and I don't remember you ever being sick." Liz waited for Sarah to say something. When Sarah did not respond, Liz said, "Is there anything you want to tell me, Sarah?"

Sarah shook her head under the intense gaze of her friend, and a tear trickled down her cheek.

"Sarah, look at me." Liz's tone was firm and yet Sarah still avoided eye contact. "You're pregnant aren't you?"

"Hush, Liz." Sarah looked up at once. "You mustn't tell anyone."

"Who am I going to tell? Of course I won't, don't be silly." Liz reached forward and wiped another tear away from Sarah's cheek with her fingers.

"Oh Liz. I don't know what to do." Sarah opened her nightstand drawer and pulled out a carefully ironed hand-kerchief that was in front of her letters.

Liz looked at Sarah's mid-section. "How far along are you?"

Sarah unfolded the cotton handkerchief and carefully dabbed the tears from her eyes. "Around three to four months, I'd say."

"Have you told John?" Liz asked.

The tears started to flow freely down Sarah's cheeks at the mention of John's name.

"He wasn't happy? Sarah, tell me what he said."

They were interrupted by a knock on the door. "I've got your dinner here." The voice was Jacob's.

Liz raced to open the door and take the dinner from Jacob. "Thank you, Jacob. I'll give the dinner to Sarah."

Jacob always liked to know everything. "What's going on in there? I heard Sarah crying. Is she all right?"

Liz took the tray from Jacob while she was stood in his way so that he couldn't see in. "She's just feeling a little sick. She'll be okay."

Jacob was moving his head from side to side trying to see around her.

"Run along now, or I'll tell your *mamm* you're making a nuisance of yourself again." Liz spoke in an extremely angry voice.

From her bed Sarah could see a glimpse of Jacob shaking his head. Liz closed the door while he was standing there.

"Put it down there please, Liz, *denke*. I can't stand the smell of it. I can't stand the thought of it."

Liz put the dinner down in the corner of the bedroom before she sat back down at the end of Sarah's bed. "Now, tell me what he said."

Sarah wiped her eyes again before she took a deep breath. "After Annie and Jessie brought me back home from the train station…"

"Yes, when they rescued you from running away with John. Go on."

It was hard for Liz to be quiet and listen because she was so used to being the one doing all the talking while Sarah was naturally much quieter.

"Well, if you be quiet I'll be able to tell you," Sarah said.

"Sorry."

"So, we arranged to meet four weeks after that. I was going on *rumspringa* to be with him. Only thing was, when I phoned him to make the final arrangements he seemed

9

different, almost disinterested. So, I didn't bring up the subject of us getting together at all and neither did he."

Liz raised her perfectly shaped *Englisch* eyebrows. "You haven't even told him about you having his baby?"

Sarah shook her head. "It's as if he's lost all interest in me. Yet, the funny thing is that he writes to me nearly every day. If he didn't write I would be sure he didn't want anymore to do with me."

Liz leaned forward in an effort to emphasize what she was about to say. "You must tell him, Sarah. You must."

"*Nee*, I won't tell him. I want him to *want* to be with me. I don't want to be with him if it's only for the sake of the *boppli.*"

Liz was, for once, silent.

Sarah took Liz's silence as a sign of disapproval of her decision. "I thought you of all people would understand. I want him to be with me because he loves me. I don't want him to be with me out of a sense of duty."

Liz pursed her lips tightly. "No, I don't understand at all. He got you into this…. I mean he needs to take responsibility for what's happened. What about financial support? You can't stay in the community. You'll have to get somewhere else to live and that'll cost money. Then you won't be able to work because you'll have the *boppli* to look after and *bopplis* are so expensive."

Even though Sarah was a little upset she couldn't help but notice that Liz started to lapse into speaking Pennsylvania Dutch, something that she hadn't uttered since she left the community quite some years ago.

Liz was right though; Sarah wouldn't be able to stay in the community. She would have to think about finding somewhere to live at some stage.

"Stop. I can't think about all that right now. Please, stop." Sarah covered her face with a pillow. It was all too much. If only she could turn back time and make a different decision and not make the foolish mistake that she had made. She had got carried away with notions of love and romance without thinking of the ramifications of her behavior. Now, the harsh reality of her actions had set in. The reality was that she had ruined her life. She couldn't even bring herself to think of how her parents would react at the news that their youngest *dochder* was to be an unmarried *mudder*.

"Sorry Sarah. I didn't mean to upset you. I'm just trying to help, that's all. Do you want me to phone him?"

Sarah laughed. "*Nee*, please don't. I don't know why you would think such a thing."

Liz gave a little giggle. "At least you seem a little happier now."

Sarah was a little happier. A little happier that she'd shared some of her burden with another person. Liz was originally Kate, Sarah's older sister's, good childhood friend but now she had become a good friend to the other sisters as well since she'd been living at their *haus*.

Hard times had caused Liz to stay with the Miller's and her stay for *'just a few weeks'* had turned into something much, much longer. Liz's stay had also caused quite a bit of friction between Liz's parents and Sarah's parents and now Liz's parents totally avoided Sarah's parents.

Sarah had also heard that Liz's parents had caused Sarah's *daed* to be called to the bishop to have a meeting about having Liz at the house. Sarah never knew what happened at that meeting or what the bishop had decided on the matter, all she knew was that Liz was still at the *haus*. It was obvious that the bishop was in agreement that Liz should stay with the Miller's, at least for the time being.

Sarah had assumed that the fact that Liz could be leaving any day, with her new job and everything, that the bishop was prepared to overlook Liz's parents objections. It seemed Liz's parents thought that the best thing for Liz would be a *shunning*, to teach her a lesson, and shock her back into the community. Sarah was sure that nothing would ever bring Liz back to the community to live her life as an Amish person.

"Well, congratulations." Liz leaned forward and gave Sarah a hug.

"*Denke*. This should be a happy time for me, shouldn't it?"

Liz smiled and reached behind her head to tie her long, bleached blonde hair into a topknot. "Lots of women in the *Englisch* world bring up children by themselves. You can do it too."

Sarah smiled, but on the inside she was not smiling. She didn't want to bring up a child by herself. She hadn't planned things this way. She wouldn't have planned to have a child out of wedlock and bring shame upon her *familye.* Every time Sarah had thought of having her own *kinner* she never once thought that she wouldn't be bringing them up within the community. She wanted to bring this child up with his or her father in the Amish community.

After speaking with John about the *Englisch* lifestyle Sarah had thought that she might like to try it, but now that she was expecting a *boppli* she really wanted to stay within the safety of the community. How would that be possible now, without a husband?

CHAPTER 3

If we confess our sins, he is faithful and just to forgive us our sins,
and to cleanse us from all unrighteousness.
1 John 1:9

OH GOTT, what have I got myself into? Please help me. Sarah had prayed forgiveness many, many times yet she still didn't feel forgiven for compromising herself with a man before marriage. She had to believe she had been forgiven by *Gott* as the Scripture said because she had confessed her sin to Him.

It will do no good to see the bishop, Sarah thought. *Even if I confess my sin to him, I still can't stay in the community and bring shame to my familye and cause gossip. I will have to leave eventually when I start getting bigger, but I will think about that later. I can't face to think about that now.*

"Come here, give me another hug." Liz leaned forward and gave Sarah another hug. "Don't look so worried everything will work out just fine."

Just then they heard a small knock on the door. Liz

sprang off the bed and slowly opened the door and saw Jacob standing there. "I heard you say, Sarah is having a *boppli*."

Sarah covered her mouth in horror. Jacob was far too young to find out about these things. He had only just turned eleven and Sarah was sure he still didn't even know how babies were made. What would he think now with her having a *boppli* and not having a husband? Sarah's situation had suddenly gone from very bad to much worse. Now her eleven-year-old *bruder* had to bear the burden of her sin. Sarah realized that this was another thing she would have to ask forgiveness for. She never thought that just one sin would not only affect her, but would have a far-reaching effect on many other people.

"Were you listening at the door?" Liz spoke quietly so Sarah's parents would not be able to hear her.

Jacob nodded.

"That is a sin, Jacob. You shouldn't listen in to other people's conversations. You will have to promise me you will not tell a living soul. Do you hear?" For some reason Jacob had always been frightened of Liz and right now Sarah knew why. She spoke in a voice much like a wicked witch out of an *Englisch* storybook. Even Sarah felt a little afraid of her at that moment. Not only did Sarah feel uncomfortable to hear Liz speak so harshly to her *bruder,* she also felt uncomfortable with hearing her make him promise something. Sarah and her siblings had been taught by their parents that their word was their promise.

"I'll tell you what. As a reward for keeping your mouth closed I'll reward you with this dinner right here." Liz picked Sarah's dinner plate full of breaded lamb and vegetables off the floor and handed it to Jacob. Even though Jacob had just eaten one dinner he looked mighty pleased to be able to eat a second one. Jacob was a typical growing boy who could never get enough food.

"Wow, I won't tell anyone. *Nee*, I won't." Jacob carefully held the full plate of food. "How did it happen?"

"Now, go to your room and eat it and you'll not ask any more questions. Then I want you to go down and take the empty plate to the kitchen and tell your *mamm* and *daed* that Sarah ate all her dinner and is feeling much, much better. All right?"

Jacob carefully took the plate from Liz. "*Jah*, Liz."

"Look me in the eye when you speak, Jacob." Liz's tone was still scary.

Jacob looked Liz straight in the eyes. "*Jah*, Liz."

Liz closed the door and slid down the back of the door to the floor and looked over at Sarah. They were both speechless at Jacob finding out about the *boppli* at such an early stage before Sarah had even told her parents.

"Do you think he'll say anything?" Liz asked.

Sarah shook her head. " He's a *gut* boy, I've never known him to lie, and he did say he wouldn't say anything. You were pretty intimidating. You had me scared."

Under normal circumstances Sarah would have been concerned that Jacob had been asked to keep something from his parents, but these weren't normal circumstances.

"Yes. I have that effect on men," Liz said.

The two girls managed to giggle even though they were both a little worried.

"I hope I haven't ruined his innocence. He probably doesn't even know how *bopplis* are made and he should think that bopplis only come to a married man and woman."

"Nonsense. Don't give it another thought. It'll do him good. He can't be brought up sheltered. It's bad enough he's Amish." Liz realized she'd said something that may be offensive to Sarah. "Oh, sorry Sarah, but you know what I mean don't you? I mean to say, he'll have to know about that sort of thing eventually. Surely he's seen the farm animals doing it."

"Hush, Liz, that's an awful thing to say."

Liz giggled. "C'mon he's eleven, he's not a baby anymore. You're just being over sensitive."

The last thing Sarah needed right now was to be told she was being over sensitive. She was living in the Amish community, had done something terrible and very soon she would be bringing shame on her whole *familye* and would have to leave the only home she'd ever known for an uncertain future and have a *boppli* to care for as well. At times Liz was just a little too much and right now Sarah just wanted to be by herself.

Liz patted Sarah on the arm. "There are other options Sarah, you don't have to keep it you know."

"What are you suggesting? Adoption?"

"Well, adoption is one option. You could go away for a while, have the baby then come back to the community and no one would ever need know."

Sarah pulled a blanket around her shoulders as a way of comforting herself from that terrible thought. "I don't think I could give my baby up."

"Even if you have to be a single parent?" Liz leaned away from Sarah a little. "I'm not trying to give you advice or tell you what to do. I wouldn't even know what I'd do in your situation. I'm just saying, you must consider every option."

Sarah had to admit it was a way that she would be able to stay in the community and not bring shame to her *familye*. Could she really let someone else raise her *boppli? Maybe the boppli would be better off in a loving familye with two parents instead of one, especially an Amish familye.* Sarah was sure she could never give her baby up, but on the other hand, she did want to do the best for the baby. "I'll give it some thought, Liz. I don't think I could do it though."

In the back of Sarah's mind she hoped that John would come back to her and that they would be a *familye* together, the two of them and the *boppli*. The only problem with that was, although they had discussed having a life together they had never spoken of children. *What if he doesn't want to have any kinner? Not all Englisch couples have kinner.*

"*Denke* for everything, Liz. Now, I think I need to try to get some sleep."

Liz leaned forward and kissed Sarah on the forehead. "Everything will be all right, you'll see."

After Liz left the room Sarah took a sip of the hot lemon drink, which was supposed to cure all ills. Now it was luke-warm, almost cold.

Sarah just wanted to close her eyes and go to sleep, but she knew the cold air whistling through the window would keep her awake and possibly give her a bad chill. She got out of bed and slowly walked toward the window to close it. As she did she looked outside and noticed how the trees were encased in a glow that came from the gaslights from the sitting room downstairs. She stood quietly and watched the moonlight dance on the fields and noticed how the wind swiftly blew some leaves lightly across the newly harvested fields. How she would miss the farm when she left. Sarah sat down on the seat underneath the window, rested her elbows on the windowsill and cradled her chin in her knuckles while she gazed at the barn and across the fields. This had been the only home she'd ever known. How could she possibly leave it?

How is Gott going to fix up this mess I've got myself into? I'm about to bring a boppli into the world with no daed and no marriage. I have to leave the Amish and live in the Englisch world. What of my parents? I've inflicted this upon them as well. Sarah took a deep breath and tried to push her worrying thoughts from her mind. *I just have to believe that Gott is going to work things out. I have to have faith and believe.*

Sarah looked out the window for a few more moments

before she took her prayer *kapp* off and changed into her nightgown. Once again she lay on her bed and pulled the photo of John out from under her pillow. How she hoped that he still loved her. After she said goodnight to him and gave the photo a little kiss she installed him back under her pillow and turned out the gas lamp next to her bed.

CHAPTER 4

AND JESUS SAID UNTO THEM, Because of your unbelief: for verily I say unto you, If ye have faith as a grain of mustard seed, ye shall say unto this mountain, Remove hence to yonder place; and it shall remove; and nothing shall be impossible unto you.

Matthew 17:19-21

THE HARDER SARAH tried to sleep the more it eluded her. She replayed the last phone conversation with John over in her head.

He had arranged for her to call him at a certain time specifically so they could make arrangements for them to meet. *So why didn't he mentioned anything about them coming together again at all? He just talked about how busy he was all the time. It's as if I just rang a friend to have a chat and pass the time,* she thought. Mentioning a baby was hardly appropriate given the tone of their conversation.

Since Sarah had already gotten permission to go on

rumspringa from her *daed* she had to tell him she was delaying it for a little while longer.

"Sarah."

Sarah opened her eyes the next morning to see Annie, one of her older sisters looking down at her. "Go away." She pulled the covers over her head hoping it wasn't time to wake up already.

"*Mamm* let you sleep in because you were sick, but she said you should be getting up by now. She needs you to help with the chores if you're feeling better."

Sarah mustered some energy, slowly pushed back the covers and sat up slowly and waited to feel sick, but nothing happened. She was tired, very tired, but today she didn't feel nauseous at all.

"You feel better?" Annie asked.

Could it be possible that this morning sickness has gone for good? Sarah hoped it had. "*Jah*, I do. I do feel better."

Annie picked a dress off the clothes peg and handed it to Sarah. "*Gut*, there's something I want to ask you."

Sarah yawned and stretched out her arms over her head. "What is it?"

"Will you be an attendant at my wedding?"

Sarah tried to do the math quickly in her head she was now roughly nearly four months and with December only being next month she would be nearly five months. She would be under closer scrutiny at a wedding and hoped the pregnancy wouldn't be showing by then. What if she had to leave the community before Annie's wedding? She said the only thing she could think to say. "I would love to. Of course I will."

Annie bounced toward the bedroom door. "*Gut*, I'm only having you as my attendant. Kate's making both our dresses, you know what I'm like at sewing – not very *gut*. She said for us both to go there this afternoon for a fitting - if you're well enough."

Sarah gave a nod thinking that it would be far better to have the fitting when she wasn't showing. Then it occurred to her, what if she couldn't fit into the dress by the time the wedding came? The only thing for it was, she had to let Kate in on the secret. That way her older *schweschder* could make the dress a little bigger to accommodate her increasing size.

~

SARAH HAD ASSUMED that they were going to Kate's home for the fitting, but found out that they were going to the tailor's where Kate worked. "We're both wearing blue." Annie said as the buggy pulled out from their *haus* on the short trip to Kate's work.

Sarah's thoughts were far from the wedding. "When?"

"The wedding, of course." Annie eyed momentarily took her eyes off the road to study her *schwescher's* face. "What's wrong with you lately? You seem so distracted and distant."

Sarah wished she could be more excited about Annie's wedding. A wedding is a very important occasion in some-one's life, but all Sarah could think of was her own sorry situation.

"Okay, now I know there's something wrong. Is it John?" Annie asked.

"Kind of." Sarah knew she'd have to tell Annie sooner or later, but wasn't quite sure if right now was the best time.

"Sarah, don't be so annoying. Are you going to make me guess?"

Sarah could see that her *schweschder* was getting agitated with her by the way she was glaring at her. "I suppose you have to find out sooner or later. I'm going to have a *boppli*." Sarah reluctantly studied her *schweschder's* face to gauge her reaction.

Annie pulled the buggy off to the side of the road and

SAMANTHA PRICE

Sarah had a tense minute until Annie finally spoke. "You're not are you?"

Sarah nodded. "*Jah*, I am."

Annie's face turned beet red with fury. "Is it John's?"

Sarah nodded.

Annie pursed her lips together, shook her head and yelled. "This never would have happened with an Amish *mann*. I was worried something like this would happen. I hoped you'd be more sensible. What were you thinking, Sarah? How could you do that?"

Sarah remained silent. She'd already gone over everything in her head a million times. Why did she keep seeing John when she found out he wasn't Amish? Why did she lie with him before marriage and go against God's laws and normal Amish behavior? Those and a hundred other questions had gone through Sarah's mind for the past few months and Sarah didn't want to go over those same questions with Annie. How could she even speak those things she felt when she was with John? How could she tell Annie that she was overcome with passion and felt that once she was in John's arms nothing else in the world had mattered? Or that she only felt truly alive when she was with him?

"Jessie and I haven't even kissed. Do you know that? Kate and Benjamin never kissed or touched either before the got married."

Sarah felt horrible at the things Annie was saying. She knew they were true though, but when she was with John it was like he was the only important thing in the world. How could she tell Annie that now when it didn't even make sense to herself?

Sarah fought back tears and wrapped the blanket that was on her knees up over her neck. She knew if just one tear escaped then she wouldn't be able to stop crying. "I can't...I can't speak about it. Not if you're going to be angry."

22

Annie was silent for a while before she said softly, "What are you going to do?"

Sarah shrugged her shoulders in reply as she had no words to express all the thoughts swirling in her head. She had no idea what she would do and couldn't face thinking about it.

Annie looked at her *schweschder's* belly. "When, what? When will he or she be coming? I mean, what's your due date?"

"I'm not sure. I haven't seen a midwife or doctor or anything. I'd say about April or May, shortly after Kate's *boppli*. Annie, let's just keep going to Kate's shop. I don't want to spoil your wedding plans or your wedding or anything."

"You haven't told *mamm* and *daed* have you?"

Sarah shook her head as she cuddled the blanket.

Annie headed the buggy to the tailor's shop where they were to have their dresses fitted for the wedding. "I'm sorry for getting upset, but I'm just finding it hard to believe, Sarah. It doesn't seem real."

Sarah touched her swollen belly underneath the blanket. *It's very real*, she thought. "I'll understand if you don't want me in the wedding. I will be a bit bigger by then and it might be noticeable."

"Of course I still want you at the wedding, but when are you going to tell people and what are you going to do?"

"I don't know, not yet." Sarah was definitely not looking forward to telling her parents that she was having a *boppli*. Sarah thought back to the day her older *schweschder* Kate announced that she and Benjamin were expecting. Their parents were overjoyed, but of course Kate and Benjamin were married so of course news of a *boppli* would be a good thing to the grandparents. Sarah knew she was not going to have the same delighted reaction and in fact, expected the opposite reaction from her parents. "The only people who know are you and Liz, oh and Jacob."

"Jacob?"

Sarah immediately regretted telling Annie that Jacob knew. That was another thing Annie would be angry about. "*Jah*, he was listening in at the door last night when I was telling Liz. Liz made him say he wouldn't tell anyone."

To Sarah's surprise Annie didn't seem too angry about Jacob finding out. All she said was, "I wish he hadn't heard about it that way."

"I don't want anyone else to find out until I've figured out what to do. I'll have to tell Kate though because she'll have to make the dress bigger. Bigger than I am now anyway."

"You should be able to hide it. They say you don't get really big with your first *boppli*. You'll probably be the same size that Kate is now, at the wedding."

"That's *gut*, you can't tell she's any bigger at all. Now you have to help me tell her."

It's such bad timing with Annie's wedding in a few weeks and my boppli coming so soon after Kate's, she thought. "Sorry, Annie. Sorry that you have to think of my problems when you should be enjoying your wedding plans."

"*Nee*, Sarah. It's me that's sorry. I've just been thinking that maybe I should've let you go away with John like you'd planned if that's where your heart lay."

Sarah pushed the blanket back over her knees and warmed her hands on the new gas heater installed in the dash. *What would my life be like right now if I'd gone away with John just like we'd planned? Where would I be now if Annie hadn't talked me in to going back home with her? Nee, it's best that it happened this way. If John has fallen out of love with me then the love wouldn't have lasted. I don't want him to know about the boppli. I want him to be with me because he loves me and not out of a sense of duty,* she thought. "Now, let's think about your wedding."

SARAH WAS QUITE nervous about telling her older *schweschder,* Kate, about her condition and hoped that Annie would help her break the news.

CHAPTER 5

This is my commandment,
that ye love one another, as I have loved you.
John 15:12

SARAH AND ANNIE scurried to the tailor's shop as fast as they could to avoid the cold air that was gushing down the street. Sarah never went to town much as she disliked the stares from *Englischers* that her Amish clothing drew.

A wave of warm air engulfed them as they entered Rebecca's small tailor's shop. Along with the warmth was a definite smell of freshly cut and laundered fabric. Sarah was pleased to be standing in warmth after being in the buggy. Even with the gas heater in the buggy the trip was too short for the heater to have time to warm the buggy up.

Sarah looked up to see that a modern electric air-conditioner was generating the warmth. Sarah considered that one good thing about living in the *Englisch* world would be to have electricity for things such as lights and heaters, especially at this time of year.

This was the first time that Sarah had been to Kate's work. The tailor's shop was quite small. While Kate and Annie talked, Sarah had a little wander around the shop. The walls were painted two different colors of purple, darker shade on the top part of the wall and the lighter purple on the bottom half of the wall.

Sarah had never seen purple walls before or any colored walls other than pale colors such as cream or ivory or even pale blue, which was favored by the Amish. The floors were polished wood, which Sarah considered would make it easy to see if any needle or pins were dropped. A large bench loomed at the front door, which divided the workroom and the reception area. A large well-used wooden table acted as a workbench where four sewing machines were installed. Sarah had never seen machines like these. They were large, and each one was a different shape.

Sarah noticed three doors at the back of the room. She looked over at her two sisters who will still talking so she opened one of the doors. It appeared to be a changing room, *most likely for people who need to try the new clothing on or have alterations*, she thought. The next door she opened was exactly the same, another changing room. The third door was slightly ajar. Sarah peered in through the door to see that it was a tiny kitchen, which was set up like a lunch or tearoom.

"What are you doing Sarah? Come over here," Kate ordered.

At that moment Rebecca, Kate's boss came through the front door. "Ah, hello you two and congratulations to you, Annie." Rebecca strode over and kissed both girls on the cheek.

Sarah and Annie had already met Rebecca at Kate's wedding.

Rebecca had what looked like a takeaway lunch in her hands. "I'll be out the back if you need me, Kate."

"*Denke*, Rebecca." Kate started taking Annie's measurements first as Sarah pushed her forward.

Once Rebecca was out of earshot, Sarah took the opportunity to tell Kate her news, helped intermittently by Annie.

Kate was noticeably shocked and quite angry, angry with John. Sarah realized she was most likely angry with her too, but she was just shooting questions at her about John.

Then Kate said the very thing Sarah didn't want to hear. "Have you thought about adoption?"

Before Sarah could respond Annie spoke on her behalf. "*Nee* Sarah could never do that."

Sarah looked at Annie quite surprised at her response since she'd never even discussed adoption with Annie, only with Liz. Why would Annie assume that she wouldn't adopt the baby out? Maybe she would if that was the best thing for the *boppli.*

Seeing that her question was not too popular Kate added, "It's just that you aren't married. Maybe the *boppli* would be better off with having two parents and a proper home."

Adoption was something that Sarah had never even thought of until Liz had mentioned it. She could adopt the *boppli* out to a good *Amish familye,* but how would she know for sure and for certain that the *boppli* would have a better life than being with her? *Maybe I haven't considered it up until now because I thought John might become my husband.* "I'll consider it, Kate."

Annie turned to look at Sarah with a look of horror across her face. "Give up your own *boppli?*"

"Annie, it's not that Sarah would want to give up her *boppli,* but if the boppli is better off in a *familye* then Sarah must consider that." Kate had always been the practical one.

Annie just shook her head at Kate's suggestion.

Kate straightened out her fabric tape measure in what looked like a nervous gesture. "You could go away somewhere, Sarah and come back after you've had the *boppli* and no one need know."

She'd already heard nearly those exact same words from Liz and now Sarah's legs went weak underneath her. She sat on the nearest chair and started crying.

"See what you've done now, Kate?" Annie knelt down next to her *schweschder* and put her arm around her. "Don't worry! You won't have to give up your *boppli.*"

Sarah choked back the tears. "I will have to do what's best for the *boppli.*"

"And that might be to stay with it's *mudder,*" Annie stated firmly while shooting a glare at Kate.

"I didn't mean to upset you, Sarah. I just thought it might be an option. I'll get you a glass of water." Kate hurried out to the tearoom.

Sarah dabbed at her eyes with a handkerchief.

Kate returned and handed Sarah a glass of cold water. "Don't worry about things for now, Sarah. I'll make the dress a little larger everywhere so you'll look just slightly bigger all over. No one will notice a thing."

"*Denke*, Kate."

Kate sat down next to Sarah. "What did the father of the *boppli* say?"

Annie who was still crouched down next to Sarah said, "Kate, leave it alone. No more questions, can't you see that you've already upset her?"

Sarah took a mouthful of the cool water. "It's all right she can ask questions, Annie. I haven't told him yet." Sarah added the word '*yet*' as she didn't want to tell Kate that she would never tell him about the *boppli. Nee*, that would mean another harsh lecture from her older *schweschder* and she was far too emotional for that.

"I don't want to upset you anymore, but I must say this. If you decide to keep the *boppli,* then the *daed* will have to help you out with money and things."

Sarah nodded in agreement just to keep Kate quiet for the moment. "Now you two think about the wedding. We didn't come here to talk about me."

While Annie and Kate fussed over which shade of blue to make the dresses in, all Sarah could think about was John. Kate had insisted that she should tell John that he would soon be a father and he would have to contribute financially, but Sarah knew this was something she would have to do all by herself – somehow.

"I've already finished the organdy apron, See?" Kate unfolded the white apron that Annie would wear over her blue wedding dress.

"*Denke*, it's lovely Kate," Annie said.

Sarah worked hard to push John out of her mind and admired Kate's sewing skills.

"And, this is Jessie's suit. I've nearly finished it except for the sleeves." Kate led Sarah and Annie over to view the suit, which was pinned to a tailor's mannequin.

"Lovely!" Annie ran her hand over the black material. "It feels so nice."

"Glad you like it." Kate said.

Sarah touched the suit as well. "You're so clever, Kate. Being able to sew so well."

"You're a very good sewer too, Sarah. Come to think of it, that would be a good income for you. You'll need money when the *boppli* comes."

Sarah was pleased that Kate didn't mention adoption any more and was speaking as if Sarah would keep her *boppli*. Even though Sarah intended to consider adoption she never thought that she would ever be able to go through with it.

Sarah pulled her mind back to what Kate had just said about sewing and thought of her previous attempts at sewing. "I might be all right at sewing, but I'm not as *gut* as you, Kate."

"Nonsense, you are quite *gut* and it's only practice. You'll improve quickly if you do a lot of it."

"Well, I guess I have to do something to get some money together. What do you suggest?" For the first time Sarah was feeling more confident. If she had a little money behind her, she would have more choices available to her.

Rebecca had been in the backroom the whole time and had overheard their whole conversation. She stepped into the shop. "I'm sorry to eavesdrop, but, Sarah, I do need someone to help for a few hours a week. It's just a small amount to start with, but it could develop into more hours, if you're interested." Rebecca was quite an attractive older lady and wore plain clothes. Sarah guessed her to be in her early fifties.

"*Jah*, I'd be very interested *denke*, but I'll need some practice first."

"The best way is feet first. You can learn on the job. Kate can show you what to do." Rebecca was a straight forward no nonsense sort of person but the sort of person who was like a kindly old aunt.

Sarah had to fight back the tears at Rebecca's kind offer. "*Denke* very much, Rebecca, that is so kind. I can start whenever you want me to." Sarah knew that the busier she was then the less time she would have to think about John.

Rebecca and Sarah agreed that she would start the very next day. Sarah was grateful that all the way home in the buggy, Annie didn't once mention her expectant condition or adoption and instead talked about the wedding and the clothes that Kate was making.

CHAPTER 6

*FOR I HAVE SAID, Mercy shall be built up for ever: thy faithfulness
shalt thou establish in the very heavens.*

Psalm 89:2

"THERE'S A LETTER FOR YOU, Sarah. When you finish reading
it you can come down and help with the dinner?"

Sarah was grateful that her parents never asked her who
was writing all the letters to her. They must have known it
was John, the man she nearly had run away with, yet they
never tried to stop her reading his letters. She had expected a
lecture at the very least. "All right, *Mamm*. I won't be long."

Sarah went into her bedroom and closed her door. Once
she hung her heavy black coat on the clothes peg she flopped
down on her bed and carefully opened the envelope.

My Dearest Sarah,

I hope you are doing well.

Sorry if I sounded a little strange when you called me on Tues-

day. I had a lot on my mind. I'm very busy at the moment and I think it's best that we delay you coming to see me.

I still love you and want to be with you it's just that there's a lot going on right now. When things have settled down a bit I'll let you know.

I miss you so much. I miss holding you and kissing you. I can't wait until you are back in my arms again. We will be together again soon.

I love you,

John.

After she'd read it a few times, Sarah carefully folded the letter and placed it back in the envelope and hid it with John's other letters in the little drawer of her nightstand. She was very disappointed that the letter was a lot shorter than his other letters. He'd also given her no news of what he'd been doing at all. She was at least a little pleased that he did say that he still loved her and they would be together soon. Still, it was hardly a letter that would encourage her to tell him of the *boppli. What possible reason would he have for putting our plans on hold? It just doesn't make sense unless he's lost interest in me and is trying not to upset me, or even trying to let me down gently.*

It was at that moment when she had closed the little drawer that Sarah realized she could not rely on John and had to rely upon herself only. She had to make some plans for the future and it was quite obvious that, for now at least, that those plans would not include John.

She would have to write back to him, but not now. Right now she had dinner to help prepare. Even though she was upset over the contents of the letter Sarah made up her mind not to show the disappointment on her face.

Sarah entered the kitchen to hear her *mamm* and Annie chattering away about what food they would cook for the wedding. The wedding was to be held right there at their *haus.*

Sarah's *mamm* looked up at her. "You look much better today. So the flu's gone?"

Annie raised her eyebrows and shot Sarah a look so her mother couldn't see. The look said, 'When are you going to tell her?'

"*Jah*, totally gone; I feel fine." Sarah had a horrible feeling that her *mamm* already knew. Her tummy was only just getting a little bigger. In the clothes she was wearing there was no way anyone would be able to notice her increased size. She sucked in her tummy as much as she could anyway, just in case.

As the smells of the cooking invaded the kitchen, Sarah was mighty pleased that the morning sickness had gone as suddenly as it had arrived. She was definitely not looking forward to telling her *mamm* and *daed* of the boppli and thought it best to wait until after Annie's wedding to tell them. Besides, they would have hundreds of guests for the wedding, which meant a lot of work so the last thing they needed on their minds was to learn of her problems.

After dinner that night, once the Scripture readings were over Sarah told her parents she would be starting part time work at the tailor's shop where Kate worked.

Her *daed* looked over the top of his glasses at her. "That's *gut*, but will you still be able to help your *mamm* with the chores?"

"*Jah*, of course. I'll only be doing a few hours a week so I'll try not let it interfere with the chores."

Sarah's *mamm* looked a little pleased. "I'm sure Annie and I will manage."

Her *daed* wasn't so pleased. "Annie will be gone soon and have her own *haus* to manage."

"It will all work out, Isaac." Sarah's *mamm* had that tone in her voice, which told her husband, in a very nice way, to hush and so no more. He quickly complied.

Sarah went to bed that night pleased that she now had

two jobs. She had the part time job at the tailor's and she would also sew quilts to sell, which was sort of like a job, she considered. It was clear to Sarah that if she made her own money she would be able to rely totally on herself and not have to contact John. Contacting John was the last thing that she wanted to do right now.

~

THE NEXT DAY, Annie took Sarah to the tailor's shop in the buggy. It was Sarah's very first day at her very first job.

"I'll show you how all the machines work in a minute, but first look at this." Kate took out a large parcel and unfolded a beautiful quilt. "I brought this quilt in to show you. I've just finished this one and I'm taking it in to sell today."

Sarah studied the soft, blue and green quilt and marveled at the detailed sewing in it. "Oh, that's so pretty. It looks just like the one that *grossmammi* made."

"*Denke.* I make these at night and sell them on consignment at the craft shop just up the road. As soon as they get to the shop they sell, usually on the very day they reach the shop. I make nearly $500. profit out of each one. The fabrics cost quite a bit and the shop takes a commission, but it still leaves me with *gut* money."

"Really? There's so much work in them though. How long does it take you to make?" Sarah studied the fine hand stitching.

"I do a few hours every night and it takes me about three weeks to make one. I make two styles all the time because I can get quicker when I know where I'm going with it."

Sarah nodded her head trying to work out how much that was per week. Whatever it was, Sarah knew that every little bit of money counted and she would do it for her boppli. "Will you show me how?"

"*Jah*, of course. That's why I brought it in to show you.

Mamm showed us how to make these when we were younger. Do you remember how to do it at all?"

"*Jah*, I think so. I remember *mamm* used to have all the ladies around to the *haus* for a quilting bee. I tried quilting a section once or twice, but it never looked like this. Mine was all puckered and crooked it looked quite awful. Yours looks so well finished and lovely."

Kate laughed. "*Denke*. It's just practice. You'll sell as many as you can make. The tourists love them. Take your time with it though. They can't be rushed all you'll get yourself into all sorts of trouble."

I can't get into any more trouble than I'm in now, Sarah thought as she ran her fingers over the fine stitching and studied the detailed pattern. "*Denke* for the *gut* idea. If you help me get the materials and pattern I will start tonight." Sarah wasn't sure if she would be able to sew them as well as Kate did, but she knew she would have to try.

"Don't start tonight. I'll show you what to do if you come to my place on Saturday afternoon. If you start off the wrong way it will be a disaster." Kate folded her quilt up and put it in a large fabric carrying bag. "Rebecca has a lot of fabrics here. When it's the lunch break you can go through and select some. I'll help you."

The few hours' work went by very quickly. Rebecca had Sarah working on straight seams so she could get used to working the electric sewing machines, which had a very different action to the treadle sewing machine she used at home.

～

SARAH WAS sure she remembered the basics about quilt making because her *mamm* used to do so much of it before her eyesight started to fail. She was grateful for anything she could learn from Kate as Kate's sewing was highly professional. "The cutting of each piece of fabric is of vital importance. They need to be perfectly matched in size, that's the basis of the quilt. If you get that wrong then the whole thing will be wrong."

That Saturday afternoon Sarah listened avidly to Kate's lessons on quilting.

"Then the pieces have to be put together with the utmost accuracy. If one small part is not aligned it will throw the whole balance of the quilt out."

Sarah couldn't help but cast her eyes around Kate's home when she should've been listening about quilt making. Hers was a real home, a perfect place to bring up children. How lucky Kate was to fall in love with a *gut mann* like Benjamin who made her a lovely *haus*. "Okay so what you're saying is you can't cut any corners and I have to pay attention to the detail of each piece all over the quilt?"

"Exactly. Detail, detail, detail and it's best not to rush, especially with your first attempt. If you go too quickly then it's easier to make mistakes, and it takes a lot more time to fix mistakes."

Sarah had never been good when something required concentration or detail. She was the sort of person who would rush something just to get it finished. "Got it, slow and steady and attention to detail."

"*Jah* and you have to keep checking everything."

Kate got down to the finer points of the sewing stitches, which Sarah realized was the easy part. The hard part would be the careful cutting out and all the preparation beforehand.

"Don't forget that cutting out is very important and use *mamm's* good fabric scissors." Kate called out to Sarah as she was driving off in the buggy.

"*Denke*, Kate. I won't forget."

CHAPTER 7

A new commandment I give unto you, That ye love one another; as I have loved you, that ye also love one another. By this shall all men know that ye are my disciples, if ye have love one to another.
John 13:34-35

ANNIE AND JESSIE had both been baptized into the faith as soon as they decided to wed and in doing so they committed themselves to live by the unwritten tradition known as the "*Ordnung.*" The *Ordnung* are the rules and regulations and expected behaviors of the Amish lifestyle.

The day of Annie's wedding had finally arrived. The two days preceding the wedding Sarah, Annie and their *mudder* had done nothing but cook for the crowds of, possibly up to three hundred people, who would be attending the wedding. So many that they would have to eat in shifts.

Hours before the ceremony the wagon pulled up with the benches that were also used for the church services. The men would arrange them for the lunch once the ceremony was finished.

Sarah was busy putting the finishing touches to all the roast chickens when she heard the rumbling of buggies that sounded like a thunderstorm. Sarah opened the window and leaned out to see dozens upon dozens of gray buggies headed for the *haus*. There were so many more buggies than there were for the usual services that were held every second Sunday, where they broke off into smaller groups. Today nearly the whole community turned up to the wedding.

Sarah closed the window and focused her attention back to the food, glad that there would be a few more ladies to arrive who would be able to help. She was grateful that her morning sickness had left her or there would have been no way she could have been around all this food and all these smells.

There were so many roast breaded stuffed chickens that she couldn't count them, buckets of hot mashed potatoes, coleslaw and apple sauce. The desserts were stacked in the utility room until after the main course was finished. There were all different sorts of pies, doughnuts and puddings. There were also several wedding cakes. Four wedding cakes were made by Sarah, two bought from the local bakers and six made by Amish women who were friends of Sarah and Annie's *mamm*.

"Sarah, there you are." Her mother bustled into the kitchen. "You go upstairs and get changed. I'll take over here.

"*Denke, Mamm.*"

Kate had only finished sewing the dress two days before the wedding. Sarah had already tried it on and found that the blue dress fitted perfectly and with the sheer, white organdy apron over the top of the dress nobody would ever be able to guess that she was expecting. Better still, being a cold day and the service held outside she may even be able to wear her black coat most of the time. Sarah slipped the blue dress over her head and as she tied the ties of the apron behind her, she stepped in front of the window. She looked down at the crowd of people.

As she stood there, she pretended that it was her wedding and that John was down there somewhere waiting to marry her. Chills ran all over her body as she felt pleasure in thinking what it would be like if John was Amish and if they were getting married in front of all their friends. Her thoughts made her happy, even if they were for a fleeting moment.

Jah, well that is never going to happen. I will never have an Amish wedding and no gut Amish mann will ever want me now. Sarah pulled her mind back to reality as she replaced her prayer *kapp* back on her head.

∼

HUNDREDS OF PEOPLE were gathered and Annie and Jessie were standing nervously before the bishop. Sarah being an attendant was standing next to Annie.

The bishop began a short talk. Usually the talks before a wedding were quite brief, but this one seemed quite long. As the bishop spoke on the sanctity of marriage and how important that commitment was, it struck Sarah once more that she would never be able to have a wedding like the weddings her two sisters had.

Annie's beautiful wedding to Jessie had just become another reminder to Sarah of the terrible mistake she'd made. She had always assumed that she would marry a hard-working *gut* Amish *mann* and they would be happy and have a large *familye* together. She'd always assumed that her *kinner* would be able to play with her siblings *kinner* just as she'd played with her own cousins growing up. Now that would never happen. Of course, she wanted a *boppli*, but not like this, not before she was married and certainly not to an *Englischer.*

She had reprimanded herself over her actions countless times and yes, she knew a man and woman should only come together under the sanctity of marriage, but she couldn't undo what she'd already done. All she could do was confess her sins to *Gott*, which she had already done many times. She knew she should confess to the bishop as well, but it was much easier just to leave the community and save her *familye* from shame and gossip.

Once the bishop was finished his talk Annie and Jessie publically stated their commitment to one another and the bishop pronounced them married before *Gott.*

With the ceremony over the guests sang some hymns.

Praise be God in the highest throne
Who has chosen us
Has put a beautiful garment on us
That we would be newborn
This is the proper wedding garment
With which God adorns his people
The wedding of the Lamb is already prepared
For the righteous to lead the way to
Rejoice all loving Christians
That God has received you
And prepared a beautiful banquet room for you
In which we shall all come

SARAH SAT at the main table at Annie's side and because she was an attendant of Annie's. Other ladies were helping to serve the food that Sarah, Annie and their *mamm* had spent, seemingly, days to prepare.

Once the first sitting of the food was finished Sarah went for a wander to walk off all the food she'd eaten so her tummy might settle a little.

"Sarah."

Sarah turned to see Ephraim striding toward her with a huge smile on his face. Ephraim was John's cousin and she hoped that he would mention John. John had stayed with Ephraim for months to try the Amish lifestyle and that's why when she first met John she didn't know he wasn't Amish.

"Hello, Ephraim."

Ephraim put his head to one side and casually placed his hands on his hips. "I hear you're sweet on my cousin, John."

Sarah couldn't respond to his question. She could tell by the mocking tone in his voice that he was not supportive of their relationship. Ephraim was a very handsome man, but Sarah considered the inside of Ephraim did not match how he appeared on the outside. Sarah wondered if vanity might have crept into his life. *Is he arrogant because he knows he is so handsome?* Sarah considered his looks to be quite similar to John, although her John was beautiful on the inside even if he wasn't Amish. John had been born Amish so Sarah thought that maybe that had something to do with his goodness.

"All right don't speak, but I know you were set to run away with him. Best that you know that he's engaged to someone else. An *Englischer.*" Ephraim studied Sarah's face obviously hoping for a reaction.

"*Nee.* That's not so." Sarah blurted her words without thinking. Seeing the look on Ephraim's face, she wished she hadn't given him the satisfaction of seeing her upset.

Ephraim laughed. "John is smart, handsome and quite wealthy. Why would he want a plain woman when he could have any *Englisch* woman he wants? He's a lot to give up you know."

Sarah searched Ephraim's face for a hint that he might be telling a fib.

"Think about this then. He's *Englisch* why would he want to tie himself to an Amish woman?"

Sarah wanted to say, *for love.* It was clear from the way

43

Ephraim spoke that he didn't even understand the concept of love. He was also speaking as if he himself found nothing appealing about an Amish woman. Sarah noticed over Ephraim's shoulder, that Liz was approaching them. Sarah was glad that their conversation would be shortly interrupted. Liz was wearing Amish clothing for the wedding that she had borrowed from Kate.

Sarah couldn't stop staring at her because she looked so very different. Gone were the tight *Englisch* clothing and the huge volume of bouncing blonde hair and in its place was a modest pale yellow dress and white apron. Her blonde locks were covered by a white prayer *kapp*. She still had her long nails, but they were devoid of bright polish. Instead of her usual heavily made up face she only had a dash of lip-gloss.

"Ephraim, come here," Liz spoke in her usual firm tone while adjusting her bleached blonde hair under her prayer *kapp*.

Sarah was surprised to see Ephraim turn and obey Liz's direction without saying anything further to Sarah. Ephraim's absence gave Sarah time to reflect on the news he had just hit her with. *Could John really be engaged? Then why did he want me to go back to Ohio with him? Maybe he has just recently become engaged and that explains why he doesn't want me to come there anymore. At least I know now what's keeping him so busy.* Sarah wanted to cry and if it hadn't been for her *boppli* she probably would have. She made the decision that she would not cry she would be strong for her baby.

After the evening hymns were over, the crowd of people had lessened and Sarah busied herself cleaning up the left over food and the dishes. Sarah looked around to see if Liz could help her as a lot of the ladies who were previously helping had gone home.

Sarah saw Liz by the barn talking to Ephraim. She studied their movements and gestures. They looked very much like they were a courting couple. She was giggling at the things he was saying and Ephraim had his arm up leaning against the barn and his body was facing Liz's. They looked like a very attractive couple together. Only thing was that Sarah didn't think much of Ephraim's character after what he said to hurt her regarding John and the hurtful things he was saying about Amish women even though he's Amish himself.

It wasn't just that he'd told her that the *mann* she was in love with was engaged, it was the fact that he had thoroughly enjoyed telling her the news. *Oh well, If anyone can handle Ephraim Zook, it's Liz,* she thought. Sarah decided to let Liz have her little flirtation and didn't call her over to help.

CHAPTER 8

There is no fear in love; but perfect love casteth out fear: because
fear hath torment.
He that feareth is not made perfect in love.
1 John 4:18

IT WAS VERY LATE when Sarah had finally retired for the
night. She changed into her cotton nightgown and sank
between the cool freshly washed sheets. Her hand went to
her belly as it did several times during the day. However,
during the day she had to be careful that no one saw her
hand naturally travel to her belly, as that was a familiar pose
of expectant *mudders*. It felt comforting, for Sarah, to have
her hand over her *boppli* whom she loved so much even
before he or she was born.

We will be okay, she said aloud to her baby. Sarah pulled
out the photograph of John underneath her pillow and
studied his face. *If it's meant to be then Gott will make a way.*
There is nothing I can do about it now; it's all been taken out of
my hands.

Dear Gott, I hand my boppli and myself over to you. Please look after us. Amen. With that prayer Sarah pushed the photo into one of his letters in the nightstand drawer and closed it, deciding not to look at his photo so much.

Sarah was not pleased to find out on her *schweschder's* wedding day that the *mann* she loved, the father of her *boppli,* was engaged to another woman. She wanted to phone John and ask him if it were true. Was he really engaged to an *Englisch* girl? However, rejection was something she could not handle right now. She would not phone him or answer any more of his letters. Weeks had gone by since she'd last phoned him and his letters kept coming. *Why would he keep writing to me if he's engaged to another?* Sarah hadn't replied to any of John's letters since she had called him on the phone. Now she was pleased with that decision.

~

As was usual at many Amish weddings, Annie and Jessie had stayed the night at Annie and Sarah's parents' *haus* as they had helped clean up until very late.

Annie offered to drive Sarah to work that day rather than Sarah drive the buggy herself.

"I'll hitch the buggy myself and you make sure I'm doing it all correctly. Then sit beside me while I drive?"

Annie was the one in the family that drove the buggy and now Sarah thought it time she learnt.

"*Jah,* all right then." Annie knew her *schweschder* would have to learn to do a lot of things herself now that she would be living at Jessie's *haus.* Even though Jessie lived on the farm next door it was still a fair distance away.

Sarah really enjoyed the few hours she worked at the tailor's as it gave her something other than herself to think about.

When Rebecca left the tailor's shop that morning to run

some errands, Sarah thought it the perfect time to have a private talk with her *schweschder*, Kate.

"Kate."

Kate looked across the worktable at her Sarah. *"Jah?"*

Sarah was nervous about what she had to say to Kate, but she had to tell someone. "At the wedding Ephraim told me that John was engaged to an *Englischer.*"

"Oh, Sarah. I'm so sorry to hear that. I didn't realize you still had hopes that you two would ever be a proper couple and get married."

Kate's words were like a heavy blow straight to Sarah's heart. Was it so unbelievable that she might marry John? Why would Kate think that there was no chance for the two of them? She was sure she hadn't said anything to make Kate think that.

Kate looked at Sarah's face. "Well, he is *Englisch,* Sarah. Even though he was born Amish he was brought up from a young age in the *Englisch* world. You told me he tried out the Amish world by living with his cousin, Ephraim, for a few months. He obviously didn't like it, did he?"

Sarah bit her lip. It was true he didn't like the Amish world at all and even told Sarah that she was living in a time warp. "But, I was willing to go with him and live as an *Englischer.* We had plans. I was going to get my GED and everything." Sarah's voice trailed off. What use was trying to convince Kate that what they had was true love? Even she was having doubts that John's affections towards her were real love. "I just feel terrible, Kate." The tears started to roll down Sarah's face.

Kate rushed to put her arms around her *schwescher.* "Everything will be all right. You'll see. Pray to *Gott* and He will sort it all out for you."

Between sobs Sarah said, "I have prayed, Kate, I have."

"You have to believe when you pray. *Gott* says in the

Gospel of Mark, *what things soever ye desire, when ye pray, believe that ye receive them, and ye shall have them."*

Sarah nodded; she wanted to believe that everything would work out well for her even though she couldn't possibly see how they would. Everything looked so bleak. She would have to start a whole new life for herself without her *familye* and without John. It sounded so easy just to believe that you can have whatever you ask for. "I just feel I've been so bad how can I ask *Gott* for something and expect Him to work things out when I got myself into this situation in the first place?"

"Sarah, all people sin. *Gott* forgives our sins, if we confess them. There is not one sin that is worse than another sin. You have asked forgiveness haven't you?"

Sarah wiped the tears off her face with the back of her hand. *"Jah."*

"Well, you've been forgiven. That's what the Bible says." Kate handed Sarah a handkerchief.

Sarah dabbed at her eyes. "Okay, *denke.* I feel a little better."

The bell of the front door, which warned them of a customer's entrance, interrupted the girls. Sarah looked up to see a tall, older Amish man then put her head down, as she didn't want to talk to anyone Amish for fear of gossip. Kate talked to the man who was looking for Rebecca.

After he left the shop Sarah asked, "Who's that?"

"That's Jeremiah. Not sure of his last name, but he comes here a bit. He's sweet on Rebecca."

The girls giggled.

"I'll put a pot of *kaffe* on for us." Kate headed to the back tearoom.

"No *kaffe* for me please." Sarah used to love *kaffe,* but she'd lost her fondness for it ever since the morning sickness had started. Her taste for everything else had returned except for the *kaffe.* "Lemon tea?"

"*Jah*, I'll make some."

Sarah could hear Kate rattling around while she was making the tea and called out to her, "Does Rebecca like him too?"

"I think so. He seems very nice." Kate brought two steaming mugs out and set one in front of Sarah.

"Get any tea on the fabric and Rebecca will most likely kill you. Tea and *kaffe* stain really badly on fabric."

Sarah laughed. "I'll be very careful. So tell me about Rebecca and Jeremiah."

"Nothing to tell really. He just started coming in here a while ago with odd sewing jobs. He's a widower and comes in to talk to her quite a bit. That's all I know." Kate took a sip of her hot drink. "She lights up though, after his visits."

Sarah smiled at the thought of love and how it could light up a person from the inside and make them feel alive. That's how she had felt with John. She felt alive when she was with him almost as if she was not really living when she was apart from him. Sarah sighed. At least she had known love in her life, something that maybe, not everyone experiences. She had to be grateful for that, at least.

CHAPTER 9

And that ye study to be quiet, and to do your own business, and to work with your own hands, as we commanded you; That ye may walk honestly toward them that are without, and that ye may have lack of nothing.
1 Thessalonians 4:11-12

SARAH ARRIVED HOME ready to tackle her new quilting venture. She had a bundle of fabric already waiting up in her room and all the instructions from Kate were firmly in her head. She decided to start that very night after the *familye* Bible readings.

As Sarah approached the front door the familiar smell of her *mudder's* fresh baked bread distracted her from her thoughts of quilting and suddenly reminded her of how hungry she was. Sarah had gone from hardly being able to eat anything at all to being quite ravenous most of the time. The feeling that she used to have at the end of every meal had now changed and she never seemed to have that feeling of fullness. She tried to curb her appetite, as she feared getting too big too soon which would jeopardize her secret.

"There's another one of those letters for you." Her *mamm* said as she opened the door.

Sarah knew, the way her *mudder* emphasized the word *those,* that she knew the letter was from John. Her parents knew John as the *Englischer* she'd nearly run away with.

"*Denke, mamm.*" Sarah, unable to stop herself went to the kitchen and cut herself a slice of bread and ate it quickly before taking the letter off the kitchen table to read in her room.

The letter was a disappointment as was every letter since she had phoned him weeks ago. There was no news of his studies, no news of the job he was to begin and certainly no news of his engagement to someone else. In fact, there was nothing about his life at all, yet his letters were still full of his love for her and promises that they would be together.

Sarah carefully folded the letter and put it with the others in the top drawer of her nightstand. There was no use even reading the letters from him anymore as they were all the same. She decided that she would just keep the letters from him in a bundle and never reply to any of them; there was clearly no point. She would put John right out of her mind and just think about herself and the *boppli.*

After dinner, Sarah had carefully cut out pieces of fabric scattered all over her bedroom floor. The only way she could accurately cut out the pieces was to sit on the floor and cut them out with her *mamm's* large scissors. She could've used the large table in the kitchen where the *familye* ate; only Sarah thought it best to keep out of her parents' way as much as possible.

As she carefully measured and drew a line where she would cut, she was sure she could feel the baby move inside her. It was like little tiny flicks, or flutters, which Sarah thought was like butterfly wings. Was she imagining it? *Is this what babies feel like when they move?* Sarah lay down on the bed so she could concentrate on what she was feeling.

As soon as Sarah lay down she had to fight the urge to sleep. She had been so tired lately. She waited for a while and nothing happened. After a few more moments of lying perfectly still Sarah felt the movements again. *That's my boppli moving.* Sarah was so excited that she just had to tell someone, but who?

Naturally the first person she wanted to tell was John, but of course, that was out of the question since she wasn't talking to him at all and he didn't even know about the *boppli.* Her parents didn't know, so she couldn't tell them. Annie was out with Jessie as she was most evenings so that left Liz. *Jah, I have to tell Liz that I just felt my boppli move.* Sarah intended to go straight to Liz's bedroom to share the news, but it was just so comfortable on the bed and she was so very tired she thought she would just lie there for just a few more moments. She was drifting off to sleep when Liz just happened to knock on her door.

"Can I come in, Sarah?" Liz asked.

Sarah jolted herself to an upright position. *"Jah,* of course."

Liz closed the door behind her. "Asleep so soon?"

"Nee, I didn't want to be. I've got so much to do tonight I'm glad you've come and got me out of bed." Sarah got off the bed and knelt down on the floor to finish cutting out while she talked to Liz. "There's not much room sorry. You can sit on the bed and talk to me if you like." Sarah looked at Liz's slim figure and felt a little envy. She knew she would get a lot larger than she was right now and she was already feeling quite chunky. Sarah picked up the scissors and started following the lines she had traced for cutting. If she were going to get this done she would have to talk and cut at the same time.

Liz stepped over the carefully cut out pieces of fabric and lay down on Sarah's bed tummy first. "Quilting, I see."

Sarah glanced up at Liz and wished she could lie on her tummy like that as well. "*Jah*, I need all the money I can get for the baby."

"Nice colors!"

"*Denke*. I have to tell you something, Liz; I'm so excited. I just felt the *boppli* move."

"Oh, Sarah, that's just sensational. What did it feel like?"

Sarah put her hand against her tummy. "It feels very strange, to have something moving inside. It feels like something soft and gentle, like butterfly wings."

"That's so nice. That also leads me to why I've come to talk to you."

"*Jah*?" Sarah realized at that moment that Liz wasn't just there for small talk. Nevertheless she returned her attention to the cutting out in front of her.

"I've made an appointment for you at my doctor for tomorrow afternoon."

"What?" Sarah almost squealed in shock and dropped the large metal scissors from her hands.

As usual when things looked like they weren't going to go her way the tone in Liz's voice turned rather stern. "You haven't seen anyone yet have you?"

Sarah realized that time was getting away and if she had already felt the baby move then maybe she should go and see someone to check that all was going okay. She never had the need to go to a doctor before in her whole life. "*Nee*, but I wasn't going to have a doctor I'm going to use a midwife. *Denke* anyway."

"Think about it, Sarah. Ephraim's mother is the midwife who everyone in the community uses. Do you want things to get back to John? Can you use her anyway if you've left the community by then?" Liz was silent for a while waiting for

Sarah to answer her questions. "Have you thought about any of these things, Sarah?"

Sarah knew she was having trouble facing the fact that time was marching on. She was already five months into her pregnancy and she wouldn't be able to stay in the community or use a midwife from the community, for that matter.

Liz's high-pitched voice was starting to irritate her, but she was thankful for her concern and knew that she had her best interests at heart. "*Denke*, Liz. What time did you make the appointment for?"

"I know you work in the mornings so I made it after I finish work too so that I can come with you. Is 4.30 okay?"

"Jah, *Denke*, so much Liz. My head's in such a muddle."

"I know; you're hopeless." Liz spoke in a kindly and affectionate tone even if her words were harsh.

Sarah deliberately turned the attention away from herself and asked Liz a few questions of her own. "I saw you and Ephraim looking pretty cozy at the wedding."

Liz looked a little embarrassed and her face flushed a shade of bright crimson. "I've liked him for a while now."

"Really? He seems to like you as well." Sarah thought them a most unlikely couple. Then again, Sarah could not see Liz with any Amish *mann* at all. The thought of Liz with an Amish *mann* was just too ridiculous. Liz wore makeup all the time, and she had bleached her already fair hair into a lighter shade of platinum blonde, her nails were usually long and brightly colored. Sometimes she even wore little patterns on her fingernails. It wasn't only her hair and makeup it was her clothes, which were very much *Englisch* and tightly fitted. She did help with the chores, but only when she was wearing big thick gloves so she wouldn't ruin her nails. *Nee, I can't see her living an Amish lifestyle at all.* The thought, at least, put a smile on Sarah's face.

Liz nodded regarding Sarah thinking Ephraim liked her, but of course, she would be used to most men liking her.

CHAPTER 10

Fear thou not; for I am with thee: be not dismayed; for I am thy God: I will strengthen thee; yea, I will help thee; yea, I will uphold thee with the right hand of my righteousness.
Isaiah 41:10

THE APPOINTMENT at the doctor was quite quick. He checked Sarah's blood pressure, took some blood to test and then set up an appointment for her to have an ultrasound.

As they were leaving the surgery Sarah turned to Liz. "*Denke*, for coming with me. I'm not too sure about having an ultrasound."

"Nonsense, everyone has one. It's perfectly safe." Liz linked her arm through Sarah's as they walked back to Liz's car. "Have you heard anymore from John?"

Sarah's heart beat a little faster at the mention of John's name. "*Jah*, most days I get a letter from him. I've stopped reading them though."

Liz just nodded her head as if she understood Sarah's

reasoning. Sarah was quite surprised as she had expected a lecture from her.

"Ephraim told me that John's engaged to someone else." The words hurt her even as she said them, but she wondered if Liz had heard any more information from Ephraim.

Liz slowly nodded her head. "I didn't know if you knew. Ephraim told me that too."

Sarah looked down at the ground as they walked.

"Engaged is not married though, there's still a chance."

Sarah shook her head and said, "I'm not going to go chase after him, Liz. If he prefers someone else, then I'm not going to stand in his way."

SARAH'S *BOPPLI* was due in three months. Sarah could not physically conceal her secret any longer and decided that she had to tell her parents that night. *After the nightly Bible reading would be the perfect timing*, she thought. All through dinner she felt sick at the thought of having to tell her parents. She knew they would be extremely upset and disappointed in her and worse, she knew she would have to leave the *haus.*

Liz wouldn't be home until later that night and there was only Jacob and her parents at dinner. As usual Jacob was sent up to bed at his eight o'clock bedtime after the readings.

As Sarah was sitting down with her parents, she knew this was the perfect time to reveal her secret. She had rehearsed what she would say so many times, yet all of those words had gone out of her mind completely. Sarah knew both her parents were going to be hugely disappointed in her. Her two older sisters had set a wonderful example of how an Amish woman should behave and Sarah had felt like she behaved the opposite to her sisters. She had let her *familye* down in so many ways.

Sarah had rehearsed this in her mind so many times that

it was now making her physically ill whenever she thought of telling them. Now, it had come to the point where she just wanted to tell them and get it over with so she wouldn't have to have the trauma of continually *thinking* about telling them. She had asked advice from her two sisters on how to break the news to them and they were of no help whatsoever. All Sarah knew was that they would both be shocked. Sarah had always been such a *gut* girl and had given them no trouble, that is, until she had met John.

Sarah took a deep breath and decided the best way would be to just plunge in feet first and say the first thing that came into her head. "*Mamm, daed,* there's something I have to tell you both."

Her *daed* put the large black Bible that was balanced on his knees on the side table next to him. Her *mamm* looked up at her from reading The Budget. Neither of them said a word. Sarah felt the weight of both sets of eyes upon her.

Sarah knew that this would not go well. "What I have to tell you is not *gut*." She looked from one parent to the other and still neither said a word and their faces were without expression. She closed her eyes for a moment then said, "I'm having a *boppli.*"

After a moment of silence her *mamm* nodded her head. "*Jah,* we know." Her *mamm* looked nervously at her husband and then added, "We were wondering how long you would wait to tell us."

Sarah could not believe that they already knew. "How did you know?"

"I knew from the time you couldn't be near the meat cooking. You also don't drink *kaffe* anymore. When I was expecting you, I could never drink *kaffe.*"

Sarah's *daed* still hadn't said a word, but Sarah could sense his stern disapproval and disappointment hung heavily in the air.

Her *mamm* started talking nervously and it seemed to

Sarah her *mamm* was afraid of what her *daed* might say. "Then you started getting bigger. We're old, but we aren't stupid."

Sarah fought back tears. She deserved whatever would happen to her. She deserved it for being so stupid to make the mistake that she made.

Her *daed* eventually spoke. "Is the father of the *boppli* the one you nearly ran away with, that John *mann*?"

Whatever does my *daed* think of me now? I've lost his respect. For him to ask that question sounds like he thinks I may have been with more than one *mann*.

"*Jah.* I've made a mess of my life. He's not going to be a part of my *boppli's* life."

"*Jah*, you made a big mistake, but everyone makes mistakes. Have you confessed your sin and asked for *Gott's* forgiveness?"

"*Jah*, I have."

"Well, *Gott* has forgiven you and will no longer hold the sin against you. You must go and speak to the bishop as well and he will decide what you must do."

"*Nee*, I can't speak to the bishop *daed*, I just can't. I have to leave home and find somewhere to live." Sarah could not go through with seeing the bishop. If she wanted to stay in the community she knew there would be a big meeting with the bishop and the elders of the church and they would decide what to do with her. If they let her stay she would have to make a public confession before the whole community. Even if she did just that, it would not stop shame coming upon her *familye*. *Nee*, she could not see that they would let her stay. There were no unwed *mudders* in the community at all. That sort of thing never happens in the Amish community.

"It won't be acceptable in the community," her *daed* said.

"You can stay here." Her *mamm* said.

"*Nee*, I can't stay and bring shame upon you. Think of all

the gossip and all the talk. *Nee*, I will not stay. You would get *shunned* for having me stay. I never intended that I would stay beyond the time when I could no longer hide it."

After a time her *daed* spoke. "That is why we stay separate from this world, so things like this cannot happen. The *Englisch* are not like us."

How could Sarah even begin to explain to her *mamm* and *daed* that she thought John *was* Amish when she first met him, he was dressed in Amish clothes and was even at the youth group, which was an Amish event. Even though she found out he was *Englisch* that very same day, by then it was too late. She'd already fallen in love. No, that was something they would never understand.

"*Nee, denke*. I must go." Sarah could not face having to speak to the bishop. Nor could she stay and risk having her parents *shunned*. "*Denke*, for not being upset with me."

"We are both very upset about it Sarah, but what's done is done. Go and wash your face ready for bed," her *mamm* said.

Sarah's *daed* cleared his throat like he did when he had something important he was about to say. "Sarah, this wouldn't have happened with an Amish *mann*. That's all I will say on the matter. You must learn from your mistakes."

"I will." Sarah kissed them both on the cheek and headed to her bedroom. It had gone better than she had thought. She expected them to yell at her or lecture her, or some sort of reprimand or her *mamm* to cry; yet none of those things happened.

Sarah noticed how her parents balanced each other perfectly. It had been clear to Sarah that her *daed* had been furious about her condition. She was sure her *mamm* had been a calming influence on him and comforted him about the situation and even made him look at in a different way.

Sarah thought that they had the ideal marriage, it was clear they both really loved each other, and they totally supported each other in everything. It was obvious that they had known about her condition for some time and had discussed it at length. *Maybe one day,* Sarah thought, *I may have a relationship like that, but having a boppli out of wedlock will make finding a gut mann a lot more difficult.*

CHAPTER 11

Finally, brethren, whatsoever things are true, whatsoever things are honest, whatsoever things are just, whatsoever things are pure, whatsoever things are lovely, whatsoever things are of good report; if there be any virtue, and if there be any praise, think on these things.
Philippians 4:8

SARAH DREADED GOING to bed because it was when she was lying in bed that she had time to think about John. During the day her work at the tailor's shop and chores filled her mind while at night she had quilting to think about, but when she turned her lamp off at night, John's face was always before her. Nothing at night could switch off her thoughts of John.

Even though she hadn't replied to the last of his letters, they had arrived just as frequently. Even though she didn't want to read them, she kept all his unread letters in a bundle under her mattress, as she couldn't bring herself to throw them away.

Why did I fall in love with an Englischer? She wondered if she should phone him and hear it from him directly that he was betrothed to someone else, or engaged as the *Englisch* say. *I could phone him and give him a chance to explain himself for the sake of the boppli.*

"*Nee*, I will not." Sarah spoke out aloud and rather frightened herself. *He deserves no chances. We had plans, real plans and he's just tossed me aside for another girl. Let him have his exciting life with this other girl. I certainly won't be calling him ever again.* Having no phone on the property, the only way they could speak was for Sarah to phone him, which she had done in the past from the phone in Jessie's barn. *He will stop writing sooner or later*, she thought.

~

AT WORK, Sarah had graduated from straight seams to doing hems on the overlocking machine. "Kate, I told *mamm* and *daed.*"

Kate looked up from the beaded *Englisch* gown she was hand-stitching diamantes on to. "How did they take it?"

Sarah had just started sewing a hem so she waited before she finished it before she spoke. "Much better than I expected. They even said I could stay there at the *haus.*"

"The bishop would never allow that, Sarah. They'd be *shunned.*"

"I know they will. I know I can't stay there, but I have decided to keep the baby."

"*Jah*, I thought you would. I suppose if you confessed to the bishop and made a public confession you would be allowed to stay at the *haus.*"

"*Nee*, I couldn't live through the shame and think of the shame for *mamm* and *daed.*" An unwed *mudder* was just unthinkable amongst the Amish. "I can't do that. *Nee*, I couldn't."

Kate straightened in her chair and picked up another diamanté to attach to the gown. "I wouldn't either if I were in your situation."

Jah, but you'd never be silly enough to be in my situation, Sarah thought.

Sarah noticed that Kate was so cold that she had a small electric heater blowing on her feet. It was then that Sarah realized she had hardly felt the cold at all in the last few weeks as the *boppli* had become like a little heater, warming her up. "Kate why are you so cold? I thought pregnancy stopped you being so cold. You're not that much further along than me."

"I'm always cold, especially my feet. I didn't have a scrap of morning sickness either and you did didn't you?"

"Jah, that's true. I guess everyone is different."

A customer who brought in some clothes that needed adjusting interrupted them. Kate showed the customer to the change room and pinned and marked the dresses ready for sewing.

Once the customer left Sarah asked. "Can you help me find somewhere to live, Kate?"

Kate sat back down at the worktable across at Sarah. "Why don't you live in Rebecca's apartment above the shop here where I used to live? It's only small, but I really loved living in it."

Sarah thought that the location would be so convenient being in the center of town with all the shops close by. She wouldn't have any transport so being so close to everything would be perfect. "Could I?"

"I don't see why not. Rebecca hasn't let it out yet. I'll ask her when she comes back."

Rebecca had left the shop to run some errands and when she came back she was delighted that Sarah was interested in the apartment.

"*Jah*, come up and see it right now. See if it suits you," Rebecca said.

Sarah knew it would suit her before she saw it.

Rebecca unlocked the door of the internal stairway and Sarah followed close behind her. "I haven't let it out yet because it needs some little things doing to it. Like a new coat of paint."

Sarah looked around the room. It was just one room, but very large. Much like her bedroom at home, it was plain and sparsely furnished. In the corner was a small kitchen sink with cupboards and a microwave oven.

In front of the kitchen sink was an old wooden dining table and four chairs. The floorboards were wide and highly polished. A large bed was flanked by two nightstands and there was a large chest of drawers against the side wall. Sarah walked over to one of the two windows in the apartment and looked down at the street below and briefly watched all the people walking about below. The apartment smelled a bit stuffy, but Sarah knew that was only because it had been locked up for sometime. "This will be *wunderbaar*, Rebecca. How much will it be?"

"Stay for nothing, Sarah. The electricity is combined with the shop below so just make a contribution to the monthly electricity."

Sarah was amazed at Rebecca's generosity and she could see why Kate felt like she was a second mother to her. "*Nee*, I couldn't do that. *Nee*, I must pay properly."

Rebecca looked into Sarah's eyes and rubbed the side of her arm. "Would you deprive me from helping you?"

Sarah just raised her eyebrows. She'd only known this type of kindness from the Amish, yet Rebecca was *Englisch* even though she had grown up Amish. Sarah remembered Kate telling her that Rebecca's *Englisch* husband had died around five or six years ago. Rebecca had left the Amish to marry Colin when she was quite young.

"*Denke*, Rebecca."

"You can pick the new color for the walls if you like." Rebecca picked up the paint chart that was on the kitchen table and pointed to a color. "I was thinking of this color." The color Rebecca pointed to was a pale yellow, almost cream color.

Sarah took the paint chart that was being handed to her. "That looks a nice color."

The walls were currently a dull gray and Sarah thought that the pale yellow would really brighten the apartment up as it had a warm looking hue rather than the starkness of the gray.

"I had the painters booked in for next month, but I'll see if they can move it forward to tomorrow. If not, I'll get someone else to do it. I'm guessing you're in kind of a hurry?"

"*Jah*, kind of." Sarah patted her tummy. "It doesn't even need to be painted, Rebecca. It's fine as it is."

"*Nee*, see there, and there?" Rebecca pointed out to Sarah all the areas where the paint was chipped or scratched. "It hasn't been painted for years and I like to try to keep it in good condition."

Sarah took one better look around the apartment. She could really see herself living there and was starting to look forward to it. Finally, things were starting to work out for her. This was the first time in quite a while she felt that something was going her way. "*Denke*, so much. Oh, I can't wait."

Rebecca opened and closed the window that overlooked the street to see that it opened and closed easily. "You can move in on Saturday if you don't mind the smell of the fresh paint."

"I'm sure I'll be all right with it."

When they both came back downstairs Sarah told Kate she would be moving in to the flat.

"I'll have Benjamin help you move your things," Kate said.

Sarah was at last pleased that she had faced up to telling all her *familye* about the boppli and now she had a place to live. That was two huge milestones out of the way. However, the fact that she would have to leave the Amish weighed heavily upon her. Being Amish was all that Sarah knew and being Amish was who she was. Yet through her mistake Sarah would almost certainly never be able to live in the community ever again. That was something that Sarah had to get used to.

CHAPTER 12

*And Jesus answering saith unto them,
Have faith in God.*
Mark 11:22

THE BISHOP HAD FINALLY SUGGESTED to Sarah's *daed* that it would be best if Liz found another place to stay. Sarah had often wondered why her *mamm* and *daed* let Liz stay for so long considering the flamboyant *Englisch* style clothing she wore, which some might consider almost provocative at times. That night she heard her *mamm* and *daed* talking on the easy chairs while she was washing up.

"She's a *gut* girl and just needs a little time to straighten herself out. Proverbs chapter twenty-two, verse six says, *Train up a child in the way he should go: and when he is old, he will not depart from it,*" her *daed* said.

Then she heard her *mudder* respond. "*Jah*, well she was brought up well."

"She will return to the Amish, you will see."

"I don't doubt it, Isaac, I don't doubt it, but we must obey what the bishop says. We've provided a place for her to stay and that is all we can do. Now it is up to *Gott*."

From the accidently overheard conversation Sarah found out that her *mamm* and *daed* expected that Liz would return to the Amish some day. That was something that Sarah seriously doubted.

Liz had been a bit sad to leave, but she found an apartment fairly quickly which wasn't far from Sarah's new apartment.

~

THE PHONE in the tailor's shop rang and Kate answered it. "Sarah, it's Liz on the phone."

"Hello, Liz."

"I'm picking you up in half an hour for the ultrasound. You didn't forget did you?"

"*Nee*, of course not." Sarah couldn't stop thinking about the ultrasound and was quite nervous about having an image taken of the *boppli*.

"I won't park the car. I'll just pull up out front and you come out when you see me, okay?"

Sarah found it quite convenient to have a friend with a car as there was nowhere to park a buggy near the ultrasound clinic. While she was staying with Sarah's *familye* Liz had to park her car behind the barn.

Liz picked Sarah up on her hour lunch break and only having part time work Sarah had finished for the day. "I'm quite nervous about this, Liz."

"There's nothing to be nervous about. It doesn't hurt or anything."

"I know, but taking a photo and everything. You know an image…"

"You want to know if the baby's healthy and everything don't you?"

Sarah put her hand on her baby and nodded.

"Well it's just modern technology, take advantage of it."

Sarah wished she could be as confident about everything as Liz was. Liz just seemed to take everything as it came and go into every situation at full steam ahead. "*Denke*, for arranging all this, Liz. I really appreciate it."

"You're welcome. You and Kate are so lucky to be having *bopplis*."

Liz's words were strange to Sarah's ears. She'd never considered herself to be lucky to be having a *boppli* at all. It was considered a blessing when a married couple were having a baby but what was it when an unwed mother was having a baby? Sarah was conflicted whether she should be pleased about it or not.

"That's a nice thing to say, Liz."

"No, I mean it. Not all women can have children at all. Maybe I might be one of those women, who knows? So when you find out you are having a baby you should celebrate whether you have a husband or not."

That's all right for Liz to say since she's an Englischer now, Sarah thought. *Englisch women might not feel the need to have a husband, but I want to have a real family. I want my children to have a mamm and a daed and a proper haus.*

～

SARAH LAY down on the examination table with Liz sitting next to her on a chair.

Sarah was already in a white hospital gown, which opened at the back.

"Now we just need to push this up." The nurse pushed the hospital gown up until Sarah's tummy was exposed. "We need to put this gel on your bare tummy."

"My, you're a lot bigger than I realized." Liz said.

The nurse squeezed the gel all over Sarah's bare tummy.

"Oh, it's so cold," Sarah said.

The nurse laughed. "Yes, sorry. I know it's cold but we need to do it so this machine can give us a proper reading." The nurse's attention was on the monitor beside her as she moved the little hand held machine all over Sarah's tummy. "Now see there? That's the heart beating."

Sarah and Liz could see a fuzzy thing on the screen, which was pulsating in and out.

"It's so amazing," Liz said.

Sarah couldn't even speak and had tears in her eyes as the reality hit her that she would soon have a real live *boppli* in her arms. She glanced at Liz and noticed she was wiping tears out of her eyes as well.

"It's sounding all healthy and good. Now here's the hand and here's the head." The nurse pointed out all the baby's features to the two girls. "Do you want to know if it's a boy or a girl?"

"Yes," Liz shouted.

"No, I don't want to know yet. No, Liz."

"All right then." Liz was noticeably disappointed.

Once the ultrasound was finished the nurse handed Sarah two black and white photos of her baby. Sarah felt a little strange having a photo as Amish don't have or take photos. However, she had a photo of the *boppli's daed* so she would keep the photos in the same envelope.

SARAH DECIDED to see Kate and tell her about the ultrasound before she went up to her apartment. Kate was still working at the tailor's.

"Sarah, there you are."

Oh no, what now? Sarah thought. "What is it?"

"Annie just phoned from Jessie's place. Annie was in Jessie's barn when the phone rang. It was John. He was looking for you. He asked Annie why you haven't written to him and wants to know if you are all right!"

Sarah found the nearest chair and sat down. "She didn't tell him did she?"

"*Nee*, of course not."

"She just said she didn't know anything about you not writing and said you were all right and she would let you know that he called."

Why is he calling when he is engaged? Maybe he wants me as well as his Englisch woman? The thought of him calling her when he was engaged to another woman made Sarah think that he was not a very *gut* type of *mann*. She wanted her *mann* to be honorable and faithful, faithful to just one woman.

"You go upstairs, Sarah. I'll bring you up a hot lemon tea as soon as Rebecca comes back. Don't worry! Everything will work out, you'll see."

Sarah trudged up the stairs. Why was her life suddenly filled with so much drama? At least she knew that her *boppli* was strong and healthy, that's all she wanted to think about for now.

～

BEING ALONE IN THE APARTMENT, Sarah was able to get so much more quilting done. The old dining table was a perfect size for cutting out all the small pieces of fabric needed for the quilting. She knew that the more she sewed the more money she could save for her *boppli*. It also meant less time thinking about John. Sarah had made and successfully sold one quilt and was starting her second one.

～

JUST AFTER OPENING the tailor's shop two mornings later, Sarah was sitting alone in the shop trying to work out why one of the machines had stopped working. She looked up at the sound of the bell over the front door and rose to her feet to greet the customer. Yet this was no customer. She found herself face to face with the very handsome, John.

CHAPTER 13

Every valley shall be exalted, and every mountain and hill shall be made low: and the crooked shall be made straight, and the rough places plain:
Isaiah 40:4

"JOHN." Sarah walked to the counter; thankful that there was no way he would be able to see the roundness of her belly under the heaviness of her black shawl.

"Hello, Sarah."

Sarah's baby seemed to wake up at the sound of his or her father's voice and kicked hard.

"What are you doing here?" She wanted to hold him, but she knew she couldn't. It was an awkward moment and was glad of the bench between the two of them. It didn't help that he was even more handsome than she had remembered.

"Why haven't you called me or written me?"

Should I tell him I know of his engagement? Or should I just tell him I don't want to see him anymore? All Sarah really wanted was to have his arms around her, yet she fought that impulse. "I phoned you remember? We arranged that I should phone you to arrange to meet."

"It was bad timing, so much has happened."

Sarah shook her head and her voice rose in volume. "I don't know why you are even here! You didn't even mention on the phone about us meeting. I'd arranged for *daed* to let me go on *rumspringa* and everything was turning out just liked we'd planned it."

"A lot's happened, Sarah. Anyway I'm here now." John reached out his hand to touch her and she pulled away.

"Do not touch me! Ephraim said that you're engaged to someone."

John hit his head and color rose to his cheeks. "What? And you believed him?"

Sarah remained silent and just looked at him waiting for some sort of an explanation – he owed her that much.

"Haven't you read any of my letters?"

"Some." Sarah didn't know if she could believe anything this *Englischer* said anyway. She thought she knew him once, but now he could easily have been a stranger. She'd heard so many negative things about people, *Englischers*, in the outside world so how could she believe anything this *mann* had to say? "Is it true?"

John smoothed one large strong hand through his dark hair. "Can we go somewhere to talk?"

"*Nee*, I can't leave the shop. I'm the only one here. Besides whatever you have to say can be said straight out, right now."

John took a deep breath and his strong shoulders lowered slightly. "When I came to the community, I was engaged to someone, that part is true. I wasn't happy. I didn't know whether it was because I should go back to my Amish roots or whether it was something else that I was dissatisfied about. The moment I met you, I knew that I couldn't marry anyone but you. I called off the engagement with Darlene the moment I got back to Ohio. There are some other things that kept me away as well."

Sarah wanted to believe what he was saying, but why had he been so distant on the phone and why was he turning up now? She wondered if he had heard about the baby. "John, so much time has past. Why have you come now?"

"Ephraim said that there's a rumor going around about you. I just have to know if it's true."

Anger rose within Sarah. Ephraim seemed to be in the middle of everything. Ephraim was the one who told her that John was engaged which caused her not to speak to John and now he has told John about the *boppli* when he was the last person she wanted to know.

"Are you having a baby?"

Sarah was disappointed that her black shawl would not be enough to hide the truth when she was asked a straight out question by the *boppli's daed.* "It's true, but I want nothing from you."

"Sarah, what do you mean you want nothing from me? I love you. Why have you changed?"

"It's not me who's changed. We had plans I was going to get my GED and go to college remember? I was to call you to arrange for us to be together and you broke those plans – well delayed them." Sarah regretted believing the words of an *Englischer.*

"I could easily say you did the same thing when you could have come with me at the train station instead of going back with Annie and Jessie, but I kept writing to you."

Sarah thought for a while about how heartbroken John would've been when she had suddenly returned home and not gone to Ohio with him as planned. From his point of view – if what he was saying was true – she was the one who had stopped writing to him. "Well, you were engaged. How would've that worked out?"

"Sarah, I don't know. All I know is that I want you with

me. You and the baby."

"*Nee*, I don't want you with me now. Not now that you've come once you've heard of the *boppli*."

John opened his mouth to say something and Sarah put her hand up firmly in front of him as a sign to hush.

"It's too late, John. Please just go." She would rather be a single parent and bring the child up alone rather than be with an *Englischer* out of obligation alone.

Sarah considered it perfect timing when Rebecca and Kate walked through the door.

John leaned over toward Sarah. "I'm in town and not leaving until you come with me."

Sarah leaned in toward him and matching his hushed tone said, "You're in for a long stay then."

John turned and walked out of the door quickly without acknowledging the two ladies who had just walked in the door.

On seeing Sarah's face and the man who had just left, Kate knew that he must have been John. "Sarah you look as pale as snow. You must sit." Kate hurried over and took Sarah by the arm and sat her down on the nearest chair. "I'll make you a hot lemon drink."

"*Denke*, Kate."

"So, that's him then?" Rebecca asked.

Sarah simply nodded and Rebecca patted her on the shoulder and said no more.

She had wanted to see John's face for so long and now she had seen him and she wished she hadn't. At last she had got her life sorted out and made some plans and no uncertain promises from an *Englischer* would ruin those plans. Sarah needed security, security for her and her *boppli*. It was obvious that he was only appearing now because he heard of the baby. She didn't want to be with him out of duty.

Kate handed Sarah the hot tea. "After work today can I come up and talk to you about an idea I've had?"

"*Jah,* of course."

After her three morning hours work in the shop, Sarah did what she always did when she finished, which was to continue sewing quilts in her apartment. She wondered what Kate would have to say to her. She hoped it would not be more about adoption. *Maybe she's found a gut familye for the boppli. Nee, she hasn't mentioned adoption since that first time.*

Kate's loud knocking on her door interrupted Sarah's thoughts.

"Come in, Kate." Sarah yelled so she wouldn't have to get off her chair. It was getting much harder for her to move around easily. "I've boiled the jug do you want lemon tea?" Sarah loved using her electric jug; it was so much quicker than the way they had to boil water back at her *mamm's* place.

"*Jah,* please. That would be nice. You sit; I'll get it for us. I know where everything is."

Sarah was thankful to keep sitting and even though Kate was a little further along than she was, Kate seemed to have much more energy. *Most likely because she has less stress than me,* Sarah thought.

A little while later, Kate brought two steaming mugs to the dining table where Sarah was sewing.

"I had a *gut* idea as I was falling to sleep last night. Since I'm only a few weeks ahead of you having the *boppli,* maybe two or three weeks, what if we both go away until the *bopplis* are born and I come back with twins?"

It took Sarah a little while to work out what Kate was suggesting. "So pretend that my *boppli* is yours and Benjamin's?"

"*Jah.*" Kate nodded and blew on her tea.

"You and Benjamin would bring my *boppli* up as your own?"

"That's right."

Sarah couldn't think of two better parents. Her own

schweschder and a *mann* who had grown up next door to her and was like an older *bruder* to her, not just a *bruder*-in-law. *Is this Gott's answer?* she thought. "You would do that Kate?"

"*Jah*, of course. You could stay in the community and see your *boppli* all the time."

Sarah wondered what it would be like to have a *boppli* and pretend it wasn't hers. How would the child feel when once he or she grew up knowing that their real *mamm* was their *ant?* There were so many things to consider. "Have you mentioned it to Benjamin?"

"*Jah*, Benjamin agrees if you are happy with it."

Sarah took a sip of tea and thought about it for a while. "*Denke*, Kate. It sounds like a very *gut* solution. I will think about it carefully. Tell Benjamin, *denke* as well."

Kate moved uncomfortably in the chair. "Don't take too long to think about it, Sarah. No one's going to believe that I have one *boppli* and then the twin another two or three weeks later. It needs to be carefully planned if we're to do this properly."

"I understand. I won't take long to think about it."

～

SARAH THOUGHT about it for the rest of the night until deciding she wouldn't be able to live with the deception. Even though she was sure Benjamin and Kate would be the very best parents in the world, she just wouldn't be able to do it. Sarah would not be able to visit the *boppli* and pretend to be nothing more than the *ant*. It was a *gut* idea of Kate's, but it was something that Sarah couldn't go through with.

What if this is what Gott wants? It's an ideal plan with Kate due nearly the same time as me and they would be wonderful parents. Sarah went to sleep that night with all the fors and againsts going around and around in her mind until she felt she was going crazy.

CHAPTER 14

A new commandment I give unto you, that ye love one another; as I
have loved you,
that ye also love one another.
John 13:33

SARAH WAS WOKEN up early in the morning by the phone in the tailor's shop ringing. It was far too early to be a customer as it was only 6.30 a.m. Sarah made it down the stairs and into the shop before the phone stopped ringing. It was Benjamin on the phone telling her that they had just had a *dochder*.

Sarah was surprised because the baby wasn't due for another three to four weeks. "Is the *boppli* alright, Benjamin?"

"*Jah.* The midwife said to take her to the hospital because she was delivering early, but the hospital said the baby appears to be full term. We must have got our dates mixed up."

"Oh that's great. Congratulations, Benjamin. When will she be home?"

"She's home now. The hospital let her go as soon as they checked that Kate and the *boppli* were fine. The midwife is going to come and check on them both every day."

As soon as Sarah hung up the phone, she phoned Liz. Liz offered to drive her over to see the baby before they both started work for the day.

As Sarah was getting ready to wait for Liz outside, it occurred to her that it couldn't have been *Gott's* plan to have Kate and Benjamin bring up her *boppli. If it had been Gott's plan then Kate would have somehow been delayed from having the boppli so soon. Nee, it's clear that was not Gott's plan for my boppli. I wonder what Gott's plan is.* Sarah was pleased that she would no longer have to struggle with the idea of her *sweschder* bringing her *boppli* up as her own. That was one less worry off her plate; however, it was one less option available to her as well.

~

"KATE." Liz yelled as she walked though the open door and proceeded straight through to Kate's bedroom. Sarah followed close behind her.

Kate was standing up changing the baby girl's nappy.

Both girls kissed and congratulated Kate.

"She's so tiny and so beautiful." Sarah said as she gazed at the tiny toes and the tiny little fingers with perfect little, miniature fingernails.

"She's gorgeous. I want to put a big pink bow in her hair," Liz said.

Kate laughed. "There'll be none of that fanciness for this little girl, besides she hardly has any hair." Kate covered her up with a small white blanket and put a little white knitted bonnet on her head to keep out the cold. "We've called her, Hannah, Hannah Elizabeth Yoder."

"After *mamm* and *grossmammi*, that's so lovely." Sarah

thought Kate to have the most wonderful life. She had the security of a *gut mann*, a *haus* and now she had a beautiful *boppli*.

"Can I hold her?" It had been a long time since Sarah had held a *boppli* and it seemed strange to her that she would suddenly have her own *boppli* to take care of.

Kate handed her to Sarah. "Mind her neck. They don't have strong necks to start with."

Liz leaned down and smelled Hannah's head. "Oh, doesn't she smell good."

Sarah smelled her as well. "*Jah,* she smells lovely. She's so cute, Kate."

Seeing Kate's tiny, new *boppli* made Sarah all the more keen for her own baby to arrive. How those last few weeks were dragging by.

"Sorry that the idea I had won't work out for you now, Sarah."

Sarah put her arm around Kate. "*Denke,* that you and Benjamin were willing to do that for me, but it obviously was not meant to be."

The next ten minutes were spent explaining to Liz the idea that Kate had about bringing up Sarah's baby as her own. Liz thought that it would have been a most suitable arrangement.

As both girls were just about to leave Kate said, "Oh Sarah, I nearly forgot. *mamm* and *daed* want you to go to dinner tomorrow night at home."

～

SARAH PULLED up in the taxi outside the *haus* that used to be hers. How odd it felt to be going there now as a visitor. It had only been a few weeks since she'd been there, but she'd forgotten, or maybe she'd never realized how truly pretty the *haus* was from the outside. It was all white and two stories high with a handsome porch running the full length of two sides of the *haus*. Some flowers were just coming into bloom now that fall was over. As Sarah stepped on the porch she noticed that it was swept clean, that was a chore that used to be hers. *Maybe Jacob is doing that now*, she thought of her young *bruder*.

"*Mamm*."

Her father yelled, "Come in. Your *mamm's* in the kitchen."

She saw her *daed* in his usual chair reading The Budget, which was the only thing she'd ever seen him read besides the Bible. "Hello *daed*, what do you think of your new grand daughter?"

Her father put his reading material down. "She's truly a blessing. She looks just the same as Kate did at that age."

Sarah was a little emotional as she wondered whether her *mamm* and *daed* would treat her child differently to Kate's child. Since her child would be born out of wedlock—and to an *Englischer*. "I'll go and help *mamm* in the kitchen."

"*Nee*, sit down I have something to say."

From the tone of his voice, Sarah knew she was here for more than just dinner. *Maybe they want to coax me to go and talk to the bishop?* Sarah sat down in one of the two big wooden chairs next to her *daed*. "What is it?"

"I'll get straight to the point. Since you won't have a wedding like your two sisters, I may as well give this to you now." Her *daed* handed her a thick envelope.

Sarah took the envelope from his hands and looked inside. She was shocked to see a bundle of cash neatly folded in two. "What is this?"

"That was to be your dowry. You have it now, to help with your *boppli*."

"*Ach, Dat*, I can't it's too much."

Her *daed* leaned forward toward her as if to emphasize his point. "Your *mamm* and I have had to save the dowry for three girls. Since there is no husband to give it to, you take it to help with your *boppli*. We want you to have it and you must take it since you won't be having a husband."

The words *won't be having a husband,* cut Sarah deeply, but it was a fact and a fact that she had to get used to. Sarah leaned forward and hugged her *daed*. "*Denke*, so much. This will help the *boppli* so much. There are so many things I need for him or her."

"Now go and help your *mamm* while I keep reading this." He smiled and held up The Budget.

After Sarah talked with her *mamm* about Kate's new *boppli*, she noticed that the *haus* was so much quieter with Liz gone. That was until Jacob came running in straight through the front door and into the kitchen.

"Sarah." He gave Sarah a hug. "You've got fat." He poked her lightly in the tummy.

"*Jah*, I'm fat all right." Sarah was not in the mood for a conversation on the reason she was fat. He had already found out some time ago that she was having a *boppli* and that's all she wanted him to know of the subject, for now.

Their *mamm* left off mashing the potatoes for a moment to scold Jacob. "Hush, Jacob. Go and talk to your *daed* while we finish dinner and take those dirty boots off at once."

"*Jah, Mamm*." Jacob turned to take his boots off at the back door.

Sarah brought the dinner plates out from the utility room and placed them on the dining table. "*Denke*, so much for the money, *Mamm*."

"You might as well put it to good use. It won't be easy bringing up a *boppli* by yourself. But, better to be by yourself than running off with an *Englischer* who might take you away from *Gott*."

Sarah had been brought up with a *mamm* and *daed* who truly loved each other. She wondered whether all Amish married couples were in love or whether they married out of convenience. *It's not like there's millions of menner to choose from like in the Englisch world*, she reasoned. She knew that Kate and Benjamin had been truly in love before they got married. Annie and Jessie were also in love, but what of other Amish couples? Sarah considered it very hard to tell whether a couple was in love or not since no Amish folk showed affection or the likes in public.

While Sarah set the table, a smile came to her face as she was reminded of some advise her *mudder* gave her years ago regarding *menner*: *If you're late getting dinner then set the table because when he walks in the door and sees that the table is set, he thinks that dinner won't be far away.* Sarah could hardly see that she would ever need to use that advice, not now. Another thing she remembered her *mamm* saying was: *If you have something important to discuss with your husband or you want to ask for something, always do it after he has had a gut meal.*

"What are you smiling at? I haven't seen you smiling much in the last few months," her *mamm* said.

"Just thinking of *menner*. Were you in love with *daed* when you married him?"

Her *mamm* took a deep breath and lowered her shoulders. "I knew your *daed* was a *gut mann* and his heart was strong in faith toward *Gott*. I also knew he was hard working. That was really all I knew of him."

Sarah stopped what she was doing and looked at her *mamm* in shock. She was sure that they would have been most deeply in love before they married. "So, you mean. You didn't love him when you got married?"

"Depends what you mean by love. I had the love of *Gott* for him as to all *Gott's* people."

"You know what I mean, *mamm*, romantic love."

"*Nee*, I think it is a mistake to wait for some giddy feeling. You want a *mann* whose heart is right toward *Gott* and who is kind and a hard worker." Her *mamm* shook her head. "I'm sorry I didn't tell you sooner. I didn't think I would need to tell you something, which to me is so obvious."

Jah, that's maybe where I went wrong. I got carried away with the notion and the feelings that John gave me rather than look for a mann who would stay with me forever. I needed to be more practical and look at my long-term future. I got carried away with romance, which isn't real. Or maybe if it is real – it doesn't last forever.

CHAPTER 15

By whom also we have access by faith into this grace wherein we stand, and rejoice in hope of the glory of God.

Romans 5:2

ONE WEEK LATER, John came to the shop again. It was early in the morning and shortly after opening time.

Both Rebecca and Kate were in the workroom sewing. Rebecca approached him when he walked through the door, and he asked to speak to Sarah.

"Just do one thing for me, please, Sarah," John said.

Sarah was embarrassed to be speaking in front of both Rebecca and Kate who could obviously hear all that they were saying. "What is it?"

"Come to dinner with me tonight so we can talk?"

Sarah thought that might be a good thing to straighten things out so he could finally go home and also so they wouldn't have to talk in front of other people. "Okay."

His blue eyes twinkled as he smiled which set Sarah's

heart racing. *Why doesn't he love me like I love him? I can't be with him now. Not like this.*

⁓

JOHN TOOK Sarah to a quiet restaurant at the edge of the town. "I need you to be straight with me, Sarah. I need to know why you keep pushing me away."

Sarah remained silent while she gathered her thoughts.

The waitress came over with the menus, but neither of them was very hungry and just ordered a salad each for them.

John waited for the waitress to leave before he spoke again. "Do you still love me?"

Sarah felt all the air leave her body as she involuntarily sighed. She couldn't say that she didn't love him. "It's not that, John. I don't want you to be with me just for the baby. I want you to love me for me. I want to be enough for you without the baby. You've only come here when you heard about the baby. You didn't come for me."

John put his hand forward to hold Sarah's, but she pulled away from his touch. "There was a reason I couldn't come here before now." John shifted in his seat and looked very uncomfortable. "I didn't want to worry you with my problems. Nor do I now."

He was disturbed about something so Sarah didn't interrupt and gave him some time to speak.

"My Mom, was sick, very sick. She passed away, and I came straight here from her funeral."

Sarah opened her mouth in shock at his devastating news. At that moment, the waitress placed bread in front of them.

John picked up a knife and buttered some bread. "Please understand, Sarah, I couldn't leave before then and I couldn't have you come to me when I was looking after my mother. I didn't want you around all that sickness. Besides that I wouldn't have been able to give you any attention."

Sarah liked the fact that John looked after his mother when she was sick. That showed her that he was a *gut mann.* She only wished that she had known that before now. "I didn't need attention, John. Anyway, why didn't you just tell me what was going on?"

John reached out to hold her hand and this time she let him. "I explained it all to you in my last few letters. When you stopped writing to me I got scared and thought I better tell you everything. At first I didn't want to burden you with my worries or problems. I'm an only child and used to doing things my way, which is usually alone."

Sarah started to make sense as she pieced all the information together. She wished she hadn't jumped to so many wrong conclusions, and now, she wished she had read his last onslaught of letters.

"How did you know where I was and know about the *boppli?*"

"Ephraim."

Sarah nodded. Of course Ephraim would have told him.

"I stopped at Ephraim's house on the way and he told me of the rumors surrounding you. He also told me where to find you. Please believe me I was on my way to come see you and take you away with me before I even knew about the baby."

Sarah studied John's face. She really wanted to believe all the things he said, but she didn't want to let herself get into a position where he would be able to hurt her again.

"I even had this for you, Sarah, from a long time ago. The day after you left me at that train station." John let go of Sarah's hand and pulled a diamond ring out of his pocket. "I bought this the day you left me at the train station. I knew we would be together one day."

Sarah looked at the ring but did not touch it even though

he was handing it out for her to take. "Oh, it's a pretty ring, John, but Amish don't wear jewelry." It had a large round diamond in the center with smaller diamonds set all the way around the band. She didn't want to seem ungrateful, but in her heart she was a plain woman and not a woman to wear jewelry of any sort. Sarah wanted a commitment from the heart not a trinket, no matter how much it cost.

John placed the ring on the table. "What are you saying? Are you going back to the community?"

Sarah nodded. "*Jah*, I think I might after the *boppli* is born. I will make a confession to the bishop and he may let me go back." Sarah doubted that would ever happen yet it was a secret hope that it just might happen.

John took hold of Sarah's hand once more. "I don't think they would let you back in, Sarah. Not from what I know about the Amish."

Sarah's eyes fell down to the food in front of her. He was most likely right, the Amish wouldn't let her back in with a *boppli* alone, but with a husband *and* a *boppli,* they just might.

"What about us, Sarah? You're the only thing that kept me going all these months when I was looking after my mother. I love you. I love you so much." He leaned over and kissed her hand that he was holding on to.

Sarah knew that John obviously couldn't be with her because of his sick mother, but he could have at least told her about it when she called him that time when they were to arrange to be together. She would have understood that he couldn't be there. At least it would have been better than wondering why he was so distant to her and trying to only guess why his letters had been so brief. "So much has happened. You abandoned me when I needed you. I've had to feel so much shame and embarrassment for being an unwed expectant mother."

"I'm here now, Sarah. I promise to never ever leave you again."

The words that John was speaking were the words that Sarah had always wanted him to say. This was everything Sarah had ever dreamt of. She knew there would be no space ever in her heart for another *mann* and her *boppli* would need two parents.

"I'll do anything, Sarah. Anything you want me to do, just say you'll be mine. Marry me?"

"Would you return to the Amish for me?"

John's face suddenly changed into a very sour expression. "I believe in God that's why I tried out living the Amish lifestyle, but it has too many rules that I couldn't make sense of or see any reason for. For example, I don't see why you have to live without electricity and work so hard."

"It's all about being separate away from the *Englisch* world. With electricity and that sort of thing come other things that may pull you away from *Gott.*"

John nodded, but Sarah could see it still didn't make any sense to him at all.

"John, my faith is important to me and I couldn't be with someone who didn't believe in *Gott.*"

"I do believe. If that is what I have to do for us to be together then yes I will even do that. I will join the Amish if we can be together."

Sarah was pleased he believed in God because they had never had any in depth conversation regarding their faith before. She assumed he did believe in *Gott* and that's why he was trying out to see if he could live like an Amish person when he was staying with his cousin, Ephraim. Sarah thought of their future together and laughed. "How about we just live very close to my *familye* to start with before we think about trying to join the community. We can take things one step at a time."

John let out a deep breath, which was more, a sigh of relief. "Yes, that would be a lot better. Say you'll marry me then? I can't lose you again."

Sarah was about to answer him when she felt her waters break. She stood up with fright and looked down to see a puddle of water underneath her and all over the restaurant chair. "My waters just broke."

John also sprang to his feet. "Is the baby coming now?"

"*Jah.*"

Nine hours later

"PUSH, SARAH, PUSH," the nurse instructed.

Sarah had no idea it would be this hard. She had rejected all the modern drugs offered by the hospital opting for a natural birth with as little intervention as possible. However, Sarah wished she had been able to have her *boppli* at home as these surroundings were sterile and cold. All Sarah could see everywhere she turned was stainless steel.

Between the contractions the nurse said, "Not long now, maybe just one more big push and you'll be done."

The next contraction came in a crescendo, and with all the strength that Sarah had she bared down and somehow managed to push the baby out. She saw a flash of pink skin and heard loud cries. The baby was immediately picked up by a nurse and wrapped in a blanket before being handed to Sarah.

"You have a very healthy baby girl." The nurse carefully lay the baby down on Sarah's chest.

"Oh, she's so beautiful." Sarah had never felt so much love in her life. She loved him when he was inside of her, but now he was out it was more real. She kept looking at her, amazed at the miracle of life. She touched her baby's hand that was outstretched and touched the soft skin of her face. The baby's eyes were open, and she was looking around the room as if she was trying to work out where she was.

"Can you let the father in now?" The nurse opened the

door and John came tumbling in as if he'd been standing against the door the whole time.

"She's a girl." Sarah said as John walked toward them.

John kissed Sarah on the cheek. "Well done, Sarah. She's just beautiful, like her mom." John stroked the baby's cheek. "I can't believe I'm a dad."

"So, this little girl interrupted you when you were about to answer my question before. Sarah Miller, will you marry me?"

Sarah turned her face up toward John. "Do you mean that?"

Sarah looked at John's face, then looked at her *boppli's* face and smiled at how similar the little one looked to her *daed*. "Yes, John Zook, I will marry you."

"Oh Sarah, you've made me the happiest most blessed man in the world. We can be a real family. You me and ... have you thought of a name?"

Sarah looked at her *boppli* to see if a name sprang to mind. "Why don't we call her after your *mamm*?"

John kissed his baby again, softly on the top of her head. "Thank you, Sarah that will be very special, Miriam Sarah Zook. My mother's name and your name; what do you think?"

"That's just perfect." Sarah never wanted to forget these special moments. She wanted to remember every little detail. It was clear that John was going to be a great father to their baby and that was something that until now, Sarah had never been sure of.

"Can I pick her up?"

Sarah laughed. "Of course; you don't have to ask me; you're her *daed*."

John sat on the edge of the hospital bed and carefully took baby Miriam from Sarah. John rocked her in his arms from side to side. "I feel I should sing a song, but I don't know any baby songs. I'll have to learn."

Sarah laughed. "I'm sure Miriam wouldn't know what a baby song was anyway."

"Look at her looking at me. She's looking right into my face."

Sarah saw that Miriam did appear to be looking straight at her father even though babies aren't supposed to be able to focus their eyes right away.

"Right now I feel like the luckiest man in the world."

"We are both very blessed, John, both of us."

"I don't think 'luck' has anything to do with it."

A tear ran down Sarah's cheek. She had a beautiful *boppli* and the *mann* she loved. It may not have happened in a perfect way, but *Gott* had forgiven her and He had made a way for her where there was no way.

~

Thank you for your interest in 'A Small Secret.'

AMISH ROMANCE SECRETS
Book 1 A Simple Choice
Book 2 Annie's Faith
Book 3 A Small Secret
Book 4 Ephraim's Chance
Book 5 A Second Chance
Book 6 Choosing Amish

If you'd like to receive Samantha Price's new release alerts add your email at:
www.samanthapriceauthor.com

OTHER BOOKS BY SAMANTHA PRICE:

Stand-Alone Christmas novel:
In Time For An Amish Christmas

AMISH MISFTIS
Book 1 The Amish Girl Who Never Belonged
Book 2 The Amish Spinster
Book 3 The Amish Bishop's Daughter
Book 4 The Amish Single Mother
Book 5 The Temporary Amish Nanny
Book 6 Jeremiah's Daughter

EXPECTANT AMISH WIDOWS
Book 1 Amish Widow's Hope
Book 2 The Pregnant Amish Widow
Book 3 Amish Widow's Faith
Book 4 Their Son's Amish Baby
Book 5 Amish Widow's Proposal
Book 6 The Pregnant Amish Nanny
Book 7 A Pregnant Widow's Amish Vacation
Book 8 The Amish Firefighter's Widow
Book 9 Amish Widow's Secret
Book 10 The Middle-Aged Amish Widow
Book 11 Amish Widow's Escape
Book 12 Amish Widow's Christmas

Book 13 Amish Widow's New Hope

Book 14 Amish Widow's Story

Book 15 Amish Widow's Decision

Book 16 Amish Widow's Trust

SEVEN AMISH BACHELORS

Book 1 The Amish Bachelor

Book 2 His Amish Romance

Book 3 Joshua's Choice

Book 4 Forbidden Amish Romance

Book 5 The Quiet Amish Bachelor

Book 6 The Determined Amish Bachelor

Book 7 Amish Bachelor's Secret

AMISH LOVE BLOOMS

Book 1 Amish Rose

Book 2 Amish Tulip

Book 3 Amish Daisy

Book 4 Amish Lily

Book 5 Amish Violet

Book 6 Amish Willow

AMISH BRIDES

Book 1 Arranged Marriage

Book 2 Falling in Love

Book 3 Finding Love

Book 4 Amish Second Loves

Book 5 Amish Silence

ETTIE SMITH AMISH MYSTERIES

Book 1 Secrets Come Home

Book 2 Amish Murder

Book 3 Murder in the Amish Bakery

Book 4 Amish Murder Too Close

Book 5 Amish Quilt Shop Mystery

Book 6 Amish Baby Mystery

Book 7 Betrayed

Book 8 Amish False Witness

Book 9 Amish Barn Murders

Book 10 Amish Christmas Mystery

Book 11 Who Killed Uncle Alfie?

Book 12 Lost: Amish Mystery

Book 13 Amish Cover-Up

Book 14 Amish Crossword Murder

Book 15 Old Promises

AMISH TWIN HEARTS

Book 1 Amish Trading Places

Book 2 Amish Truth Be Told

Book 3 The Big Beautiful Amish Woman

Book 4 The Amish Widow and the Millionaire

AMISH WEDDING SEASON

Book 1 Impossible Love

Book 2 Love at First

Book 3 Faith's Love

Book 4 The Trials of Mrs. Fisher

Book 5 A Simple Change

AMISH SECRET WIDOWS' SOCIETY (Cozy Mystery Series)

Book 1 The Amish Widow

Book 2 Hidden

Book 3 Accused

Book 4 Amish Regrets

Book 5 Amish House of Secrets

Book 6 Amish Undercover

Book 7 Amish Breaking Point

Book 8 Plain Murder

Book 9 Plain Wrong

Book 10 Amish Mystery: That Which Was Lost

ABOUT THE AUTHOR

Samantha Price is a best selling author who knew she wanted to become a writer at the age of seven, while her grandmother read to her Peter Rabbit in the sun room. Her writing is clean and wholesome, with more than a dash of sweetness. Though she has penned over eighty Amish Romance and Amish Mystery books, Samantha is just as in love today with exploring the spiritual and emotional journeys of her characters as she was the day she first put pen to paper. Samantha lives in a quaint Victorian cottage with three rambunctious dogs.

www.samanthapriceauthor.com
samanthaprice333@gmail.com
www.facebook.com/SamanthaPriceAuthor
Follow Samantha Price on BookBub
Twitter @ AmishRomance

Made in the USA
San Bernardino, CA
03 June 2018